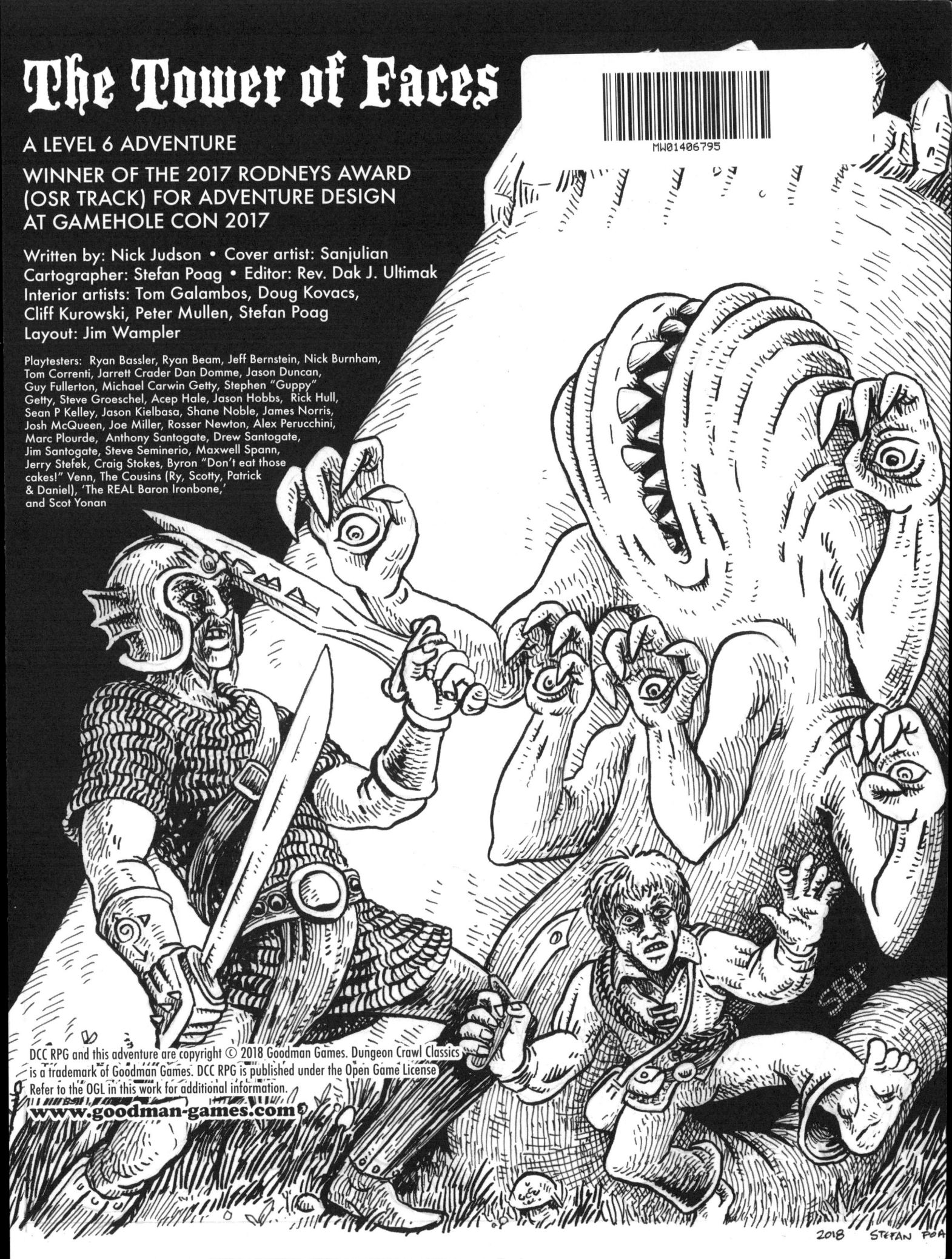

The Tower of Faces

A LEVEL 6 ADVENTURE

WINNER OF THE 2017 RODNEYS AWARD
(OSR TRACK) FOR ADVENTURE DESIGN
AT GAMEHOLE CON 2017

Written by: Nick Judson • **Cover artist:** Sanjulian
Cartographer: Stefan Poag • **Editor:** Rev. Dak J. Ultimak
Interior artists: Tom Galambos, Doug Kovacs,
Cliff Kurowski, Peter Mullen, Stefan Poag
Layout: Jim Wampler

Playtesters: Ryan Bassler, Ryan Beam, Jeff Bernstein, Nick Burnham, Tom Correnti, Jarrett Crader Dan Domme, Jason Duncan, Guy Fullerton, Michael Carwin Getty, Stephen "Guppy" Getty, Steve Groeschel, Acep Hale, Jason Hobbs, Rick Hull, Sean P Kelley, Jason Kielbasa, Shane Noble, James Norris, Josh McQueen, Joe Miller, Rosser Newton, Alex Perucchini, Marc Plourde, Anthony Santogate, Drew Santogate, Jim Santogate, Steve Seminerio, Maxwell Spann, Jerry Stefek, Craig Stokes, Byron "Don't eat those cakes!" Venn, The Cousins (Ry, Scotty, Patrick & Daniel), 'The REAL Baron Ironbone,' and Scot Yonan

DCC RPG and this adventure are copyright © 2018 Goodman Games. Dungeon Crawl Classics is a trademark of Goodman Games. DCC RPG is published under the Open Game License Refer to the OGL in this work for additional information.

www.goodman-games.com

INTRODUCTION

The Tower of Faces was selected as the winner of the Rodneys Design Award, OSR track, at Gamehole Con 2016. Goodman Games is proud to have the opportunity to publish this exciting adventure! If you are a fan of old-school gaming, we strongly encourage you to check out Gamehole Con. Held in November of every year, Gamehole Con is a rapidly growing event located in Wisconsin, ground zero of RPG gaming.

This adventure isn't a traditional dungeon delve – it's an adventure where the characters are summoned to guard and serve Yonaxis the Magnificent. As a result, this module doesn't focus on exploration (although there are areas to explore) – rather it requires the players to navigate several encounters with a wide range of unusual characters. (Many of these encounters may be determined by Random Die Drop Encounter Generator, see page 23.) Put another way, the Tower of Faces celebrates the unusual, sometimes humorous, other times deadly, daily lives of those who serve a mighty wizard.

Due to the nature of Naos – a powerful and cosmopolitan magical city – the cost and use of gold pieces in the module may be higher than what's typical in your campaign. If that's true, simply use silver pieces whenever gold pieces are noted to bring the economics of Naos in closer alignment to your campaign.

ADVENTURE BACKGROUND

For the past decade the fabled city of Naos, the necropolis of the Chaos Kings, has been attacked at random by denizens from Limbo. Coming through magical gates above the city, they've come to the city with a singular purpose: to devour anything and everything in their path.

On some days they've come by the hundreds, and in others by the thousands. Dubbed the "Chaos Maulers" no two of the denizens from Limbo have ever looked the same – except for having massive maws filled with countless teeth. When they appear the gluttonous host is always a bizarre assortment of fiends – made from a random collection of eyes, wings, claws, tentacles, and of course, their toothy jaws, which are often too large for their bodies.

Being a city of great size and power Naos has always brushed off these raids with relative ease. The city's formidable Reaper Guard (and the considerable defenses brought to bear by the noble houses) have decimated every raid in a single day. While many have complained about the raids, the Imvisible Council has done nothing to prevent them. The cynical might add that nothing has been done because the very lords of the city have profited very nicely from the attacks. For after each raid the merchants raise their prices to predatory levels, and in turn taxes gathered by the city also increase. In short, the raids from Limbo have been a boon to many a lord's coffers.

But one of Naos' famous wizards finally decided to do something about the raids when a most anticipated delivery was devoured by the Chaos Maulers. More specifically, four months ago the chimeric horrors destroyed a caravan carrying 128 drams of aged Draglic oil. Unfortunately for Limbo, that caravan was destined for the Tower of Faces – home of Yonaxis the Magnificent.

A venerable mage with puissance few dare test (except the chaos mages, and his ancient enemies, who have an annoying proclivity for vengeance), Yonaxis is known as an even-keeled wizard, with a droll and (some would whisper) annoying monotone. But in reality the mage is a passionate sort, especially when it comes to the culinary arts. In fact, Yonaxis planned to debut the complicated, yet delectable, Spotted Bog Cow Three Ways at the upcoming Sprint Solstice Soiree. (Without Draglic oil the fare is uneatable and even poisonous, causing uncontrollable gastric distress to whoever dares consume it without the prerequisite ingredient.)

So it's understandable that when Yonaxis saw his caravan devoured, on his own property, he became overcome with rage. Although the battle was short, he found little satisfaction in viewing the smoldering corpses dotting his lawn. In fact, the foul tentacles of paranoia began to tug at his fears. What if this should happen again? Were these invasions merely a plot to prevent the world from sampling his culinary delights? Yonaxis would not allow it. That day he became obsessed with finding a way to halt the raids, once and for all.

After researching the problem for months, Yonaxis found the answer: all that would be required is summoning the Fesprul. Known by sages as "The Devourer of Gates," the greater daemon from Pandemonium feeds upon the magical gates that commonly appear there. With its endless appetite for gate magic, Yonaxis knew that summoning the Fesprul would halt Limbo's invasion forever more.

With the solution at hand, Yonaxis directed his minions to execute several tasks – the last of which was to summon the Secret Guardians of Bast's Temple. Their power would be needed to protect the tower and the wizards while they cast the five-day summoning spell.

Due to the nature of city of Naos, casting summoning spells is particularly difficult. (See The City of Naos, pages 3 and 4, for more details). That's why it will take the wizards five days to summon the Fesprul. It's also why his apprentices failed in summoning the guardians, and brought the PCs instead, as well as two very angry demons. To make matters worse, the spell failed to bind the new guardians into the wizards' service, and as a result, Sorshine and Snass must negotiate with the PCs to get them to agree to guard the tower.

ADVENTURE OUTLINE

To get the most out of the module, it's recommended that it be run over several sessions – as there are numerous encounters possible each game day. An outline of the encounters for each day and night, is presented below. Encounters noted with "*" are essential to the main narrative of the adventure; the encounters where the PCs collect items needed for the final encounter, and one very dangerous assassination attempt. The other items are optional, but encouraged, as they represent a variety of interesting role playing and combat encounters for the players. Additional encounters can be generated using the Random Die Drop Encounter Generator found in the back of this adventure.

THE DELIVERIES

In this adventure the PCs will need to collect and put away three deliveries. These items will be used by Yonaxis to summon the Fesprul. The table on the next page indicates when each item will be delivered, the page number that describes each encounter and where the PCs are supposed to bring them. Note: Unless the PCs question Sorshine or Snass about the deliveries, they will not instruct them where they should bring each item – nor the fact the doors will automatically open when presented with each item. More details regarding the deliveries are also noted in the ledger (Handout E on page 23).

Page 2

ADVENTURE OUTLINE

Day 1 Encounter A: Arrival & Demons*

Day 1 Encounter B: The Anvil Contest*

Day 1 Encounter C: Obot the Albino Fence

Night 1 Encounter A: Lady Nigella Arrives

Day 2 Encounter A: Honeycakes & Ash Trolls*

Day 2 Encounter B: Veronica Offers Potions

Night 2 Encounter A: Release the Hound

Day 3 Encounter A: One Eye Morty

Day 3 Encounter B: Cursed Nirb

Day 3 Encounter C: Reaper Arrives*

Night 3 Encounter A: Aspect of Cthulhu (or see note below)**

Day 4 Encounter A: DARE Arrives

Day 4 Encounter B: Delivering the Prisoner Xoxoz the Malevolent*

Night 4 Encounter A: Wickstrom the Chandler*

Night 4 Encounter B: Breakout!*

Day 5: Encounter A: Yonaxis Summons the Fesprul*

*Indicates required events.

**If the players do not purchase the Elder Sign from Morty on Day 3-A you may skip the Night 3-A encounter, use the Random Die Drop Encounter Generator, have the weskeebs attempt to steal something from the party, or perhaps have Nigella cause trouble (if you used that encounter).

BACKGROUND ON THE SETTING: THE CITY OF NAOS

Several millennia ago the floating city of Naos was home to the dreaded Chaos Kings. Arbiters of ruin and misery, the Kings enslaved countless civilizations for their nefarious purposes. To stop them, the Lords of Law and Neutrality made a pact, and after a great war, the Chaos Kings were vanquished. To ensure the taint of their necropolis would be contained, the High Mages from the College of Arcanus and their legions of apprentices cast a mighty spell, which banished the city to a forgotten land in a shadow dimension. As a reward for their service the Lords sequestered the high mages to be stewards of the city forever more. (A map of Naos isn't provided in Tower of Faces as the focus of the module is for the PCs to stay within the estate of Yonaxis the Magnificent.)

Due to the apocalyptic nature of Naos' rebirth, a rip was torn through the very fabric of reality, and it became porous to both the neutral and lower planes of existence. As a result, the city poses dangers to visitors in three important ways:

1. All visitors (except natives) have a difficult, if not impossible time traversing the city streets. As a result, walking the streets is difficult indeed. Those who fail a DC 15 Willpower save become confused for 1d6 turns. However, wearing specially made ruby goggles (that can be bought for 5000 gp) one can see normally and not be affected by the weird nature of the city.

2. The second danger are Naos's deadly random street encounters. Visitors to Naos who are not protected by one of the Noble Houses, Guilds, Temples or Wizard Towers have a 30% chance per day of being enslaved (75%) or killed (25%) by an Outer-planar creature.

3. The third danger is related to summoning spells (Animal, Monster, and Demon, etc.). All such spells have an increased chance of failure. Upon casting a summoning spell, the natural roll is compared to table on the following page. (Note: Natural rolls of 10 or less will fail or have another effect, while rolls of 11 or higher succeed, only then do they add their spell check modifiers.)

THE ESTATE OF YONAXIS THE MAGNIFICENT

The estate of Yonaxis the Magnificent was once beautiful with artful landscape architecture featuring perfectly trimmed trees, bushes, Doric columns and fountains. Today only the tower, one tree, a shrine dedicated to the wizard's hound Crash, a Reaper's Perch (for the large messenger's birds) and a cottage remains. The grounds look like a warzone due to wizard's unwelcome visitors.

The Estate Entrance: The archway at the entrance to Yonaxis' property has no gate. In Naos no holding of a noble, wizard, or cleric may be barred.

The Outer Wall: Yonaxix's property is surrounded by a 15' tall wall covered in razor vines that are slippery (-10 on climb roll checks) and dangerous to climb. Every foot ascended results in the climber taking d8 damage.

THE DELIVERIES

Item	When the item is delivered	Page No.	Where should it be put away?
Bronze Anvil	Day 1-B. The Anvil Contest	8	To the Dwarf Door
Honeycakes	Day 2-A. Honeycakes & Ash Trolls	9	The Baker's Door
Candles of Myrrh	Night 4-A. Wickstrom the Chandler	15	The Wizard Door

SUMMONING SPELLS

Roll   Result

1   Failure and Worse! (per regular spell table.) Spell is not lost.

2   Spell summons 1d8 different creatures and also brings forth d6 demons, the later of which will attack the caster. None of these beings are bound to serve the caster and the spell lasts 1d10 days.

3   Spell summons 1d6 different creatures than intended, who are not bound to serve the caster. The spell lasts 1d4 days

4-5   Spell summons 1d4 different creatures than intended and lasts 1d8 turns.

6-10   Failure, but spell is not lost.

11-15   Spell casts as normal (include spell check modifier for spell result).

16+   Spell casts as normal (include spell check mod) and the duration lasts an additional 1d4 turns.

Area 1 - The Tower of Faces: The Tower is 50' tall and made of black glass. Ghostly faces of those imprisoned within the Tower randomly appear on its surface. Five doors (described below) surround the circumference of the tower. Its surface is also electrified; touching the tower causes 6d10 damage (DC 18 Reflex save for half damage).

THE TOWER'S DOORS

Note: All doors have an AC of 18 and 200 hps and a Fort save of +15. The interiors beyond the doors are not provided and are left for the judge to expand on their own (see adventure map).

Area A - The Dragon Door (Main entrance): A large dragon's mouth is open revealing a set of black doors with wizard runes etched across the border. There are two rings to open the door. The door is magically locked. Proclaiming, "In the name of Yonaxis the Magnificent" will open the door. The first failed attempt to open the door will result in it biting (+8 melee) for 4d4 points of damage. Subsequent failures result in a 10d6 Lightning Bolt (DC 18 Reflex save for half damage).

Area B - The Minotaur Door (The prison): Immediately left of the Dragon Door, a door bears the large face of a bull with statues of minotaurs to its right and left. The face has a large nose ring. To open this door, one must flash something red before it (causing the mouth to growl) and then pull the nose ring. Within lies an extra-dimensional prison. Minotaurs work in this chamber. Beyond the chamber there is a bridge that leads into a dimension that is home to a large maze. There are eight such bridges from locations across the multiverse. A failed attempt to open the door results in the Minotaur Door ramming all those standing in front of it. This attack does 8d6 damage (DC 18 Reflex save for half damage). When the PCs bring the prisoner Xoxoz, the minotaur statues will take hold of the prisoner, open the door and put him inside. This happens quickly, and the door is closed immediately after. If PCs should try to enter the prison they will be attacked by the statues.

Minotaur Statues (2): Init +8; Atk; battleaxe +8 melee (1d10+4); AC 18; HD 6d8+6; hp 30; MV 30'; Act 2d20; SP never surprised; SV Fort +6, Ref +8, Will +2; AL N.

Area C - The Dwarf Door (The smithy): This door bears a dwarven smith who holds a hammer. To open, one must put a piece of gold or other precious metal near its nose. In addition, presenting the bronze anvil will cause the doors to open. Small iron dwarves work in this chamber, fabricating materials for the mage and his research. When PCs bring the anvil to the door the constructs come out)side, take it and then close door.

Failed attempts to open the door results in the PCs being attacked by the dwarf's maul (+8 melee) which does 3d6+8 damage.

Area D - The Wizard's Door (Storage for magical components): This door bears the face of an old wizard with a long beard and a large pointy hat. To open this door, one must pull the beard or present the Candles of Myrrh. Doing so causes the wizard to open his mouth and reveal a door that opens to a chamber with glass gnomes working in an alchemist lab and library.

A failed attempt to open the door results in the players being polymorphed into frogs for 1 turn (unless a successful DC 18 Willpower save is made. A second failed attempt results in a 10d6 Fireball exploding at point blank range. Subsequent, failed attempts result in 11d6, 12d6, etc. fireballs. The Wizard's Door is immune to fire, and thus takes no damage from the point blank fireballs. PCs who succeed against a DC 18 Reflex save will take half damage from the fireballs.

Area E - The Baker's Door (The bakery/ kitchen of the tower): This door to the right of the Dragon Door is behind the face of a female halfling with large cheeks and a baker's hat. To open the door, one must present a tasty treat such as a box of honeycakes. Doing so causes the mouth to open and reveal a kitchen with several small copper halflings at work cooking.

A failed attempt to open the door results in (a) the nose shooting a massive amount of grease covering the PCs (b) the mouth blowing and covering the PCs in feathers and (c) the eyes shooting fire causing 3d6+3 damage, plus d6 damage per round for 1d6 rounds. A DC 18 Reflex save indicates the PC has successfully dodged these attacks.

Area 2 - The Cottage: To the northwest of the tower is a small cottage with a thatch roof. However, opening the doors will reveal a large and opulent mansion, with a steaming pool at the entrance surrounded by a gallery, dining area and kitchen. Two staircases lead to the second floor, which has ten well-furnished bedrooms. All of which have water closets, and running water. One of these rooms has a wardrobe covered in an intricate maze pattern. Within this wardrobe is a secret door, which is locked (DC 20 pick locks check to unlock) and leads to a magical portal that is connected to Yonaxis' bedroom in his tower. The cottage kitchen features a cornucopia of items sure to sate any appetite. The cottage is managed by Pricilla, a human looking golem made of iron. Pricilla wears a yellow cape, and a steward uniform. She is a perfect servant; patient, and committed to meet the needs of those who come to the cottage. When greeting the PCs she will note that special accommodations have been made (given the expectation that the PCs are the Guardians of Bast) to meet their needs. For example, she has gathered 12 artisan cheeses and four chilled silver pitchers of four different types of milk (cow, goat, camel and sheep). Pricilla is an up talker; every sentences ends in a crescendo.

Area 3 - Crash's Shrine: To the northeast of the tower there is a large black marble obelisk. This is a shrine devoted to Yonaxis' hound Crash. The face of the obelisk is covered in a bas-relief showing a hound in a number of scenes, fighting foes, sleeping, playing, etc. The obelisk is an illusion, hiding the entrance to Crash's lair, which is protected by a Ghoul Angel. More details are provided in Night 2 Encounter A: Release the Hound on page 10.

Area 4 - The Weskeebs Tree: To the west of the tower (location 4 on the map), there is a large tree with silver leaves and fuzzy green apples. This tree is home to a family of 40 weskeebs. A weskeeb is a one-foot-tall green weasel-like creature with small antlers and a monkey tail. They can become invisible and teleport at will. These friendly, but mischievous creatures love to steal from visitors (and have a +8 on all such checks). Apples from their tree heal 3d4 hit points but require a DC 15 Fortitude save when eaten. A failed saving throw indicates the individual is drunk for 6 turns and suffers -4 to their Agility and a -2 to all attacks. If an offering is left at the tree, a single apple can be taken freely. Without an offering, the weskeebs throw leaves at the thieves. Anyone approaching the tree will hear the weskeebs chittering sing-song voice. If a non chaotic PC should approach one of their apples, one of the creatures will appear before the individual, and indicate their expectations (through chittering and pantomime that something must be given before taking an apple). If a chaotic being should attempt to take an apple the weskeebs will attack. The weskeebs vocabulary is very limited. Examples of these words and corresponding definitions are below.

Term	Translation
Shine shine	a gift / treasure/apples
Chime yim	food
Hiss hiss	enemy
Luv buv	friend / mate/ family
Oy yoo	hello, greeting
Hi hi	morning / sunshine
Ni no	night / darkness
Spee spee	fun / sleep
Pow yow	Yonaxis, and wizards in general
Bi bhi	good
Yik ni	bad
Hiss zow	danger, hide quickly
Chip chip	follow

Weskeebs: Init +5; Atk bite -1 melee (1d3) or razor leaves +5 missile fire (1d3+itch poison); AC 15; HD 2d8; hp 8; MV 60'; Act 2d20; SP invisibility, limited teleportation (within 100 yards of the tree) at will, immune to poison, pick pockets are made at a +5 check; SV Fort +5, Ref +5, Will +1; AL L.

When needed, weskeebs prefer to throw leaves at their enemies from the safety of their tree. In addition to causing 1d3 damage, being hit by these leaves requires the target to make a DC 15 Fort save. Those who fail will be overcome with an intense need to itch. This condition reduces movement to 0, armor class by 4, and all attacks suffer a -2 penalty for 2d4 rounds.

Area 5 – Moat Guardians: The tower is also surrounded by a moat with purple tinted crystal water of unknown depth connected to the Plane of Water. Anything that attempts to cross the moat by any means (except for those using the bridge) will instantly cause a random encounter with one of its bound guardians. Roll 1d4, then consult the following list:

Moat Guardians:

1. Giant Emerald Octopus: Init +0; Atk tentacle +3 melee (2 plus grasp) and beak +4 melee (1d8); AC 15; HD 6d8; hp 35; MV walk 20' or swim 50'; Act 8d20; SP grasp 2 damage, camouflage; SV Fort +2, Ref -2, Will +2; AL N.

The giant emerald octopus is a native of the Plane of Water. Its tentacles and beak are covered in emeralds. In combat, they lash out with 8 tentacles, all of which can attack in a single round. The octopus will typically attack a single creature with all its tentacles, then hold down that creature and bite it.

For each tentacle that strikes the same character, the octopus receives 1d4 on an opposed Strength check to hold the character down. For example, if 6 tentacles hit a character in a single round, the character takes 12 points of damage, and the octopus roll 6d4 on a Strength check against the character. If the octopus wins the Strength check, the character is grappled and cannot attack unless he spends the next round struggling and succeeds on an opposed Strength check.

The octopus is roughly 30' in diameter in size.

2. Sea Fae Knight: Init +4; Atk trident +4 melee (1d10 + poison); AC 18; HD 8d10; hp 50; MV 20' or swim 40'; Act 2d20; SP poison (DC 15 Fort save or sleep 1d4 turns); SV Fort +3, Ref -1, Will +3; AL C.

The sea fae knight arises from the moat resplendent in silver armor and a full helm wielding a large coral trident, and wearing a cape of bubbles. His cape allows him to walk water and attack those around the moat with ease. After vanquishing the trespassers, the knight will take the slept opponents under the waves, in giant bubbles, to his hidden palace to be slaves until the end of their days.

3. Walfuss the Monitor: Init +2; Atk tusks +3 melee (2d12); AC 16; HD 8d10; hp 55; MV walk 10' swim 20; Act 1d24; SP detect enemy, gaze causes charm (DC 16 Will save to resist); SV Fort +4, Ref 0, Will +4; AL L.

Walfus is a 20' long purple walrus with golden glittery eyes. His tusks are long and sharp. When he arises from the moat he will charm the trespasser. Beings that are chaotic will be forced to jump into the moat. All others will be slept, and spend an hour daydreaming about a purple land, filled with creatures of the sea that fly instead of swimming among coral castles. If the charm fails, Walfus will attack with his considerable tusks.

4. Sicklefin school: Init +3; Atk fins +3 melee (1d6); AC 13; HD 4d8; hp 22; MV swim 30'; Act 10d20; SP swarm; SV Fort +2, Ref +0, Will -2; AL N.

The Sicklefins are thin fish that are saucer shaped with skin made of iron. Their edges are as very sharp. The school attacks in concert by swimming directly at and through their opponent. Those that are killed are summarily eaten.

Page 5

wielder's natural rate of healing is doubled. In addition, the wielder recovers twice as many hit points as usual whenever a cleric lays hands upon them.

Area 7 - The Chaos Mists: On the property there are five areas with an immobile red mist. The mists are what remains from previously slain Chaos Mist Wyrms, who were sent to assassinate Yonaxis. The red mists remain and mark where each creature was destroyed. If a character should touch this substance, they will gain a minor corruption. Roll on the minor corruption table (DCC RPG rulebook, page 116) to determine what happens to any who are foolish enough to explore them. If a PC walks near any of the mists a hand will emerge from within and gesture to the character to enter. They will also hear, "help me, help me!," in a desperate voice.

Area 8 - Reaper's Perch: 20 yards to the southwest of Dragon Door there is a 15' tall column that supports a 10' diameter platform. This is the Reaper's Perch – to accommodate deliveries from the Reapers who serve as guards and messengers to the lords of Naos. There is also a rope ladder connected to the platform that reaches the ground. On top of the platform there is a trough that is magically chilled and contains several three-foot-long fish, to feed the Reaper's mount, whenever it should visit.

THE ADVENTURE BEGINS

Day 1 Encounter A – Arrival & Demons: In the shadowy corner of a tavern, your band celebrates the spoils won from an ancient crypt. A heavy, capped, ancient horn filled with 1,000 platinum coins is your most worthy prize.

Suddenly, your revelry is cut short by the sound of thunder — and in seconds you are whisked away. Before you there is a 50' tall round tower made of black glass. Countless faces swirl in and out of view upon its Stygian surface. A moat surrounds the tower, and a stone bridge provides the only means to access it. Standing in front of the bridge and 30' away you are two identical twins wearing hooded blue robes. One of them steps forward to speak, but when he does, you hear the sound of thunder again, and suddenly two foul creatures appear before you, stinking of brimstone. *Roll for initiative!*

The two demons, noted below, attack immediately. Due to being disoriented they have a -5 penalty to their initiative roll for the first round of combat. For reference, the X on the main map indicates where the PCs first appear.

Nobryth (Type III Demon): Init +4; Atk claw +9 melee (1d6+6) and bite +9 melee (1d12+6 acid); AC 18; HD 8d12; hp 72; MV 30'; Act 2d20; SP ESP, detect good, demon traits, 25% magic resistance; SV Fort +8, Ref +10, Will +8; AL C.

The Nobryth is a seven-foot-tall black alligator with a stunted tail. It has three red eyes, large clawed hands and stands on bird legs.

V'rog (Type II Demon): Init +2; Atk claws +9 melee (1d8) and sting +8 melee (3d6 + poison DC 14 Fort save or sleep for d10 rounds); AC 16; HD 8d12; hp 66; MV 40'; Act 3d20; SP ESP, Infravision; 25% magic resistance; SV Fort +8, Ref +8, Will +6; AL C.

The V'rog is a 6' tall bipedal albino frog with black eyes, and a toothy maw. It has two arms that end in sharp blades. It also has scorpion tail.

If slain, each demon will disintegrate in a fiery cloud of ash and leave behind an oily stain on the ground.

Area 6 - "Storm Fang:" A giant spear, "Storm Fang," is embedded in the ground about 30 yards to the north east of the entrance to the estate (item 6 on the map). This is the weapon of the defeated thunder giant Elesues who previously tried to assassinated Yonaxis. To extract the spear from the ground requires a DC 25 Strength check. If a Lawful being attempts to pull out the spear he will take 2d6 electricity damage (no save), and every round they hold the weapon. To wield the spear requires a Strength of 16 (wielding it with a lesser strength will result in a -2 penalty to both attack and damage). Once removed, if the 10' spear is used in combat, it will bestow a +1 bonus to attacks and damage. In addition, it delivers 1d8 + 1d4 electricity damage on a successful strike, and crits on an attack score of 19-20.

Storm Fang the Great Spear: +1 (1d8+1d4 electricity); communicates via empathy; Intelligence 10.

Banes: Neutralization against demons and Lawful creatures; after a direct hit, the spear prevents a demon from using one of its natural powers (as determined by judge) for one full day; if bane does not have any specific natural powers spear gives victim a cumulative -1 attack.

Berserker fury when facing lawful beings; ego check or wielder gains +4 Strength and Stamina for 2d6 rounds, then is exhausted at -4 Strength and Stamina for 1d6 turns thereafter.

Special Purpose: To slay Lawful dragons.

Special Power: Regenerator. When wielding this spear, the

At the conclusion of the battle you see the two robed figures arguing. Realizing the battle is over, they look up, and then the one on the right says, "Come forward and bow and show your obedience to your Masters."

The PCs are under no compulsion to walk forward and bow. The summoning spell merely brought the PCs (who were not the target of the spell originally) to the tower; they are not bound to serve the wizards.

If the PCs ignore or react negatively to the demand, the figure who did not engage the PCs looks down and shakes his head. The other man's face turns red, and then he says, "I command you to come forward!"

When the PCs fail to do as they are commanded, the two figures exchange heated whispers. Eventually, the other one pulls a pair of goggles from a satchel, and puts them on. The goggles have purple lenses, and a silver frame. After putting on the goggles he scans the PCs, and then says:

Well hello there. It seems there has been a mistake. We intended to summon the Guardians from the Secret Temple of Bast…. Somehow you were summoned instead. These goggles tell me you are powerful "heroes" from beyond and are enemies of the forces of evil and Chaos… so perhaps we can come to some arrangement?

My name is Sorshine, and this is Snass my lesser. We are wizards, and we serve Yonaxis the Magnificent. You are on his estate, within City of Naos and this is the Tower of Faces, he says, gesturing to the black tower behind him.

The reason for casting the summoning spell is because we need guardians to protect the us, and collect certain important deliveries while we cast a powerful spell to protect the city. The spell will take five days to cast. Will you help us?

At this point, the wizards will negotiate with the PCs to serve Yonaxis. Initially Sorshine will try to tug on the PCs' heart strings, by sharing details about the Chaos Maulers, and how they're a great evil that have destroyed countless lives. If the PCs are recalcitrant, Sorshine will offer them 1,000 gp a piece for their five days of service. Failing that, he will offer up up to 1,000 platinum plus a potion of flying. (Depending on your campaign, the wizard may also offer to enchant a magic weapon. As part of this last step of negotiation Sorshine will remind the PCs they are stuck at the tower for five days – and given that, wouldn't they prefer to profit from their stay?

After the PCs agree to serve, Sorshine says, *I am glad we've come to an agreement. Here is what you must do:*

First, for the next five days you must protect myself, Snass, and our master Yonaxis from any irritation, assault or assassination. You must ensure that no one enters the Dragon Door, which is the main entrance to the tower. Sorshine turns behind him and points across the moat, to the door in question.

Beyond this, you have two other duties: first, we are expecting three deliveries. The ledger in my satchel lists those items and contains the funds to pay for them. Second, visitors may come to the tower to have their baubles identified. The charge for this service is 1,000 gold pieces. You must collect payment prior to using these Goggles of Mystical Discovery* to identify the items, he says, gesturing to goggles on his face. When you identify an item you must log the name of the owner and indicate what, if any, powers the item has in the log sheet within the satchel.

A few last words:

• *Do not swim or jump across the moat, and do not climb the tower.*

• *If you should require sustenance, a bath or use of a privy, you may use the guesthouse.*

• *Avoid the red mists on the property!*

Sorshine turns to the tower and speaks: "Master, any final words for your servants?"

The Goggles of Mystical Discovery are magical goggles that enable any thief, wizard, elf, or halfling to discern the nature of any magical item or individual, including powers, command words (if applicable) and value. However, each time this item is used the wearer must make a DC 18 Fortitude save. Those who fail will be struck by a migraine that lasts for 2d4 turns, and causes -3 on all rolls made during this time. A roll of a 1, the wearer will suffer some form of corruption.

Roll 1d100: (01-75) Minor, (76-90) Major, or (91-100) Greater. Next roll on the appropriate table (5-3, 5-4 or 5-5) in the DCC RPG Rulebook to determine the nature of the corruption. Finally, those who succeed their saving throw are left feeling irritable and have a -3 on Willpower saves for the next 2d4 rounds.

Page 7

Suddenly, the faces swirling on the faces of the tower disappear, and a face replaces it covering its entire surface. The face is of an an old man with a pointed beard who is wearing a skullcap with ram horns. He then speaks: "Guardians from beyond, Yonaxis welcomes you, and hopes you hold no resentment to this conscription. Further he promises that if you serve the tower well, and survive, you will be rewarded appropriately. So shields high–and protect the wizards!"

Immediately after Yonaxis speaks these words, his face vanishes from the tower, and the other faces swirl in and out of view upon its surface.

Sorshine then says: "We must go now to aid our master. Any final questions before we leave?"

Sorshine has little patience – and will stay only a short while. (Snass will mumble sarcastic jibes during these interactions). After the PCs ask their questions Sorshine will grab Snass, bid the PCs good luck and farewell, and then magically teleport back to the tower.

What if the Dragon Door is breached? If the Dragon Door is opened, one would see the mage Yonaxis, Sorshine and Snass working together to cast a complicated spell. The three stand in a magic circle–around them the space is warped. Alien, evil-sounding whispers can be heard. Sorshine and Snass are covered in sweat. Yonaxis looks serious, yet does not look fatigued.

When the door is opened, initiative should be rolled; the wizards gain a +3 bonus on their initiative roll. For their first action, Sorshine casts Paralysis at the lead intruder while Snass casts Hepsoj's Fecund Fungi from a scroll. Yonaxis will cast Lightening. More information about these wizards is found on page 18.

Day 1 Encounter B – The Anvil Contest: Shortly after arriving, three figures walk up the path; two dwarven brothers Borlin and Morlin carry a bronze anvil. Behind them is a large human named Ferron who also carries a bronze anvil. They are all blacksmiths wearing ruby goggles. They've come to the tower to deliver an anvil per the specific requirements given by Snass (and indicated in Handout E on page 23). Unfortunately, they don't know this is a contest, and both parties expect to be paid.

If asked, they produce the same instructions to build a bronze anvil. It's up to the PCs to determine which of the two is best. PCs who use diplomacy will prevent the situation from becoming ugly. (Both sides will threaten fines from the Blacksmith Guild, etc.)

To determine the quality of each, the PCs may use the Goggles of Mystical Discovery, or use a DC 18 Intelligence check to tell the difference between the two anvils. Both are similar quality–but the dwarven anvil is embellished–which was not required per the instructions. Thus, the human-made anvil is superior based on Snass's specifications. Note: dwarf PCs and PCs with a blacksmith background have a +3 to the roll to discern there is no difference between the two anvils, except for the embellishment provided by the dwarves.

The winner expects to be paid 1,000 gp.

Once the PCs secure the anvil, they should bring the item to the Dwarf Door. Presenting the anvil to the door causes it to open. Inside dwarven golems work as blacksmiths on various projects. They will stop shortly after the door opens, go outside, take the anvil and then return to their shop closing the door behind them. After the door closes, the area above the Dwarf Door suddenly glows with golden light, and then it quickly travels up the tower and becomes a beam of light that pierces the sky. The beam of light will stay until the end of adventure.

NPC Profiles:

Borlin the Lawful Dwarf Blacksmith: Confident and boastful, Borlin has very bad breath from chewing raw garlic, his favorite snack.

Borlin: Init +1; Atk battleaxe +4 melee (1d10); AC 14; HD1d8; hp 7; MV 20'; Act 1d20; SV Fort+2, Ref +1, Will +0; AL L. Equipment: Coin purse with 200 gp, 11sp, 3 cp. Raw garlic and small sharp knife.

Morlin the Lawful Dwarf Blacksmith (1st level): Younger of the two twins, Morlin is quiet, except when a truth must be spoken to challenge or correct a lie or obfuscation. To cover his brother's stench, he wears a derby covered in sweet smelling flowers.

Morlin: Init +1; Atk warhammer +4 melee (1d8); AC 13; HD1d8; hp 6; MV 20'; Act 1d20; SV Fort+2, Ref +1, Will +0; AL L. Equipment: Coin purse with 120 gp, 5sp, 5 cp.

Ferron the Human Warrior/Blacksmith Lawful Warrior (1st level): A tall and muscular human, Ferron is a perfectionist, who speaks with a mumbling voice due to a massive scare across his mouth. He is well groomed, and his hands are clean.

Ferron: Init +0; Atk longsword +4 melee (1d8+1); AC 16; HD2d8; hp 12; MV 20'; Act 1d20; SV Fort+3, Ref +0, Will +0; AL L. Equipment: Coin purse with 10 gp, 25sp, 10 cp.

Day 1 Encounter C: Obot the Albino Fence: A man with horrible burns on his face wearing ruby goggles comes walking through the front gate. His name is Obot the Fence. He's a member of the Sticky Fingers Guild AKA The Thieves Guild of Naos.

Obot wants several items identified, and will claim he has an arrangement with Snass; typically, he is only charged 500 gp per item identified, and in return Snass receives a 25% discount on items he desires to buy. If he can't get this price from the PCs he will leave. Items include:

Gem of the Fire Warrior: The command word to summon the fire warrior is "FeeeelaBoosh." Value: 3,000 gp.

Fire Warrior: Init +2; Atk longsword +3 melee (1d8+1d4 fire); AC 14; HD 4d8; hp 28; MV 15'; Act 2d20; SP immune to fire damage, un-dead traits; SV Fort +4, Ref +1, Will +0; AL C. Can be used once a week; summoning last 2d4 turns.

Ring of Bone: Grants +3 to AC; Using the command word "Bone Thrall" causes the wearer's flesh to become transparent (granting +5 to stealth checks) and allows communing with Aseja, a greater demon. The demon's areas of expertise include monster zombie construction, bone magic, and details regarding the Crypt of the Ghoul Mother. Value: 4,000 gp. Each time the ring is used the wearer must roll a d20; a roll of a 1 indicates an infection by spell corruption. (See page 116 in the DCC RPG rulebook for details.)

Scroll of Earth Elemental Summoning: Upon summoning, the creature is bound to serve the reader for 3 turns. Value: 4,000 gp.

Elemental, Earth: Init +4; Atk slam +12 melee (4d6); AC 20; HD 12d8; hp 48; MV 30' or dig 30'; Act 1d20 (or more); SP elemental traits; SV Fort +10, Ref +4, Will +8; AL N.

Obot: Init +4; Atk scimitar +4 melee (1d8+2); AC 13; HD 3d8; hp 20; MV 20'; Act 1d20; SV Fort +0, Ref +3, Will +1; AL C. Equipment: Mirror (hand-sized), comb, iron crowbar, fine suit of clothes, coin purse with 2 100 gp gems, 25 sp, 15 cp.

NPC Profile: Obot is an ugly vain, amoral man who collects women's hair, which he uses to make women's wigs. To compensate for his hideous looks he wears garish jewelry.

Night 1 Encounter A – Lady Nigella Arrives: A large carriage led by two grey-speckled stallions approaches at dusk. There are six guards on top of the carriage and three inside with Lady Nigella Mercer, the only daughter and heir to Duke Reginald & Duchess Fiona Mercer. The heraldry of the house is three platinum coins over a golden stag upon black, chased in silver. The guards wear ruby goggles.

As Nigella leaves the carriage, she announces that she's ready to start her training and directs the PCs to help with the luggage, which includes three wardrobes of fine clothing and two large chests with books on magic.

Nigella is at the tower per the direction from her mother, the Duchess. Unbeknownst to anyone, the Duchess made a deal with Snass for Nigella's apprenticeship. She has brought her payment for the first year of apprenticeship (four 1,000 gp gems and 200 platinum pieces)

Nigella wears a +1 magic short sword, which provides the power to make her invisible until she attacks or at will. She uses this ability when bored, and to support her kleptomania. She also carries thieves tools tools and five gems worth 100 gp each.

The PCs may possibly turn Nigella away – but they'll need a very compelling argument to do so. If the PCs accept payment, Nigella will accept the comfortable lodging within the cottage on the property, and expect at least an hour of wizardly instruction each day.

Nigella: Init +2; Atk short sword +4 melee (1d6+1) AC 14; HD 2d8; hp 10; MV 20'; Act 1d20; SP invisibility (through magic short sword); SV Fort +1, Ref +2, Will +2; AL L. Equipment: magic short sword, coin purse: (1 gem worth 1,000 gp), thieves' tools, boxes of old books, a fine wardrobe, comb, mirror and perfume.

NPC Profile: Nigella is a bright, articulate and precocious young woman, who only respects nobles and wizards. All others she treats as her lesser. She is also a kleptomaniac.

Day 2 Encounter A – Honeycakes & Ash Trolls: Ms. Haley Ninsmen, a halfling, has come to the tower to deliver her famous honeycakes. She arrives, rolling up the path inside a magic crate that tumbles across the ground. As she rolls in, she yells, "Heeeelp meeee! I've brought the honeycakes! The beasts are going to eat me–Heeelp!"

Running after Ms. Haley are five black Ash Trolls. These beasts (Grim, Scorn, Grul, Srake, Fek, and Rog) are loyal servants of House Gorfax and wear that heraldry on tabards over breastplates –a black wolf crushing a skull upon a red field. They also wear iron caps and wield two-handed swords in one hand and a shield in the other. Upon entry of the grounds, they proclaim their lord demands recompense because of the trespass from the "crate walker." The trolls speak perfect common and are polite initially, but threaten violence if the PCs prevent them from taking the crate. The honeycakes are acceptable payment, which they will request. Otherwise the trolls will accept 2,000 gp.

Page 9

Ash Trolls (5): Init +6; Atk bite +10 melee (2d8+6) or two handed sword +8 melee (1d10+6); AC 21; HD 8d8+6; hp 38 each; MV 40'; Act 2d20; SP regeneration (1d6 hp/round), immune to critical hits, immune to mind-affecting spells, immune to fire, vulnerable to water; SV Fort +10, Ref +5, Will +8; AL C.

Ash trolls are magically created beings made from the ash of trolls – which makes them immune to fire, but vulnerable to water. Further, the creatures regenerate 1d6 hit points a round. To stop the regeneration ability requires dousing the troll in water.

After the PCs overcome or use diplomacy to neutralize the trolls, the crate opens, and Ms. Haley walks out with a locked case. She requests payment prior to handing over the box (6,000 gp). She warns against opening it, or they will find it impossible to resist eating all of the honeycakes. Inside the box, there are thirteen fist-sized pastries that are gold brown with a honey glaze, and filled with a dollop of Zanzizar Honey. If challenged about the price of the cakes, Ms. Haley explains the danger collecting the honey from the great Cliff Wasps of Zanzizar. (The harvesting process requires her family to climb the cliffs in moonlight, during the last days of winter, the only time the wasps sleep. Once at the nest they then must insert metal tubes into the hive, which they heat slowly and melt the honey to cause it to drip into pots below. Not only is the climb dangerous, but if the wasps should wake, death is a certainty because of their lethal sting.)

If the PCs open the box of honeycakes, they must make a DC 18 Willpower save or be driven to devour the treats. With the honeycake box in hand, the PCs should bring them to the Baker's Door. If they do so, it will automatically open and halfling golems made from wood will emerge and take the box, and then return to the kitchen and close the door immediately after. After the door closes, the area above the Baker's Door suddenly glows with golden light, and then it quickly travels up the tower and becomes a beam of light that pierces the sky. The beam of light will stay until the end of adventure.

Note: If the PCs opt to fight and kill the trolls, 4d6 ash trolls will return later that evening to seek revenge on behalf of their lord.

Haley Ninsmen: Init +2; Atk dagger +1 melee (1d4); AC 12; HD 1d8; hp 4; MV 30'; Act 1d20; SV Fort +1, Ref +2, Will +2; AL L. Equipment: Bakers outfit, baking supplies, small bag of pastries, leather purse with 432 gp, 12 sp, and 22 cp.

NPC Profile: Ms. Haley Ninsmen is a goodhearted and expert baker. She is also an excellent businesswoman.

Day 2 Encounter B – Veronica Offers Potions: A well dressed thief with flaming red hair wearing ruby goggles walks up the path and asks the PCs if they'd be interested in buying four potions, no questions asked for 4,000 gp. (She doesn't know what the potions do because she stole them from Fogu the goblin alchemist. Each vial is marked with his sigil – a circle with four fangs).

1. Giant Slug Potion: This potion transforms the imbiber into a man-sized slug. The slug is AC 15, can spit acid (1d12 damage, attack bonus based on the imbiber), and enables the spider climbing ability. The potion is grey and white in color, thick in texture, smells like wet earth, and tastes like a slimy mushroom. The potion's effect lasts for 4d4 turns.

2. Disease Potion: This flask is filled with black and gray water with floating particles. (Upon imbibing, it has a 35% chance to cause a disease that reduces all physical stats by 3 for a week.)

3. Vomit Potion: This potion is a poison that causes vomiting. The liquid is yellow with black spots, clear texture, tastes like grass, and smells like pickles. The potion's effect lasts for 4d4 turns.

4. Fly Form Potion: This potion imbues the imbiber with fly wings. In addition to giving the ability of flight (MV 50') and spider climb, the imbiber is struck with an insatiable hunger for carrion. The liquid is black in color and filled with tiny flies. The texture is chunky and tastes horrible, but has no smell. The potion's effect lasts for 4d4 turns.

Veronica: Init +2; Atk short sword +1 melee (1d6); AC 14; HD 3d8; hp 12; MV 30'; Act 1d20; SV Fort +1, Ref +2, Will +2; AL L. Equipment: 500 gp gem (hidden isn boot), thieves' tools, ball of string, coin purse (50 gp, 32 sp, 25 cp).

NPC Profile: Veronica is a freelance thief, with a stoic demeanor who is also an obsessive compulsive. She is romantically attracted to halflings.

Night 2 Encounter A – Release the Hound: Very late on the second night the Dragon Door opens, and Snass runs out, with his face pale and covered in sweat. He immediately yells for the PCs to wake:

Servants, attend! We are being assaulted from the Astral Mists. The Master commands you to release his faithful hound Crash. Only he can protect us – so we can continue to cast our spell. Go now to Crash's shrine, on the north east of the property and free him. Tell the hound "Yonaxis is in peril in the mists." After making his desperate plea, Snass turns on his heel and runs back into the tower, through the Dragon Door.

Crash's Lair: On the north east of the property there is a large black marble obelisk. This is a shrine devoted to Yonaxis' hound Crash. The face of the obelisk is covered in a bas-relief showing a hound in a number of scenes, fighting foes, sleeping, playing, etc. The obelisk is an illusion, hiding the entrance to Crash's lair, which is protected by a Ghoul Angel.

The Ghoul Angel is a seven-foot-tall emaciated being with yellowed, withered skin. It has unusually long arms ending in dirty clawed hands. Its face has two empty eye sockets, three nostril slits, and a toothy maw with misshapen teeth. On its arms and legs there is an arcane script that binds the creature to protect the entrance. In addition, on its back there are two rotten angel wings, which are extended. The creature stands perfectly still – and will only animate and attack if someone touches it or tries to pass into the lair beyond. Note: If any Lawful or Neutral cleric attempts to turn the Ghoul Angel they will receive a +5 on their roll.

Ghoul Angel: Init +4; Atk bite +4 melee (1d12) and claws +2 melee (1d8+paralyzation); AC 16; HD 6d12; hp 36; MV 30', 15' flying; Act 3d20; SP un-dead traits, paralyzation, infravision, immune to magic missiles; SV Fort +3, Ref +0, Will +0; AL C.

A man-type creature bitten by a ghoul must make a DC 14 Willpower save or be paralyzed, unable to move or take any physical action for 1d6 hours. Elves are not affected by this paralyzation. A creature killed by a ghoul is usually eaten. Those not eaten arise as ghouls on the next full moon unless the corpse is blessed.

Crash's Lair

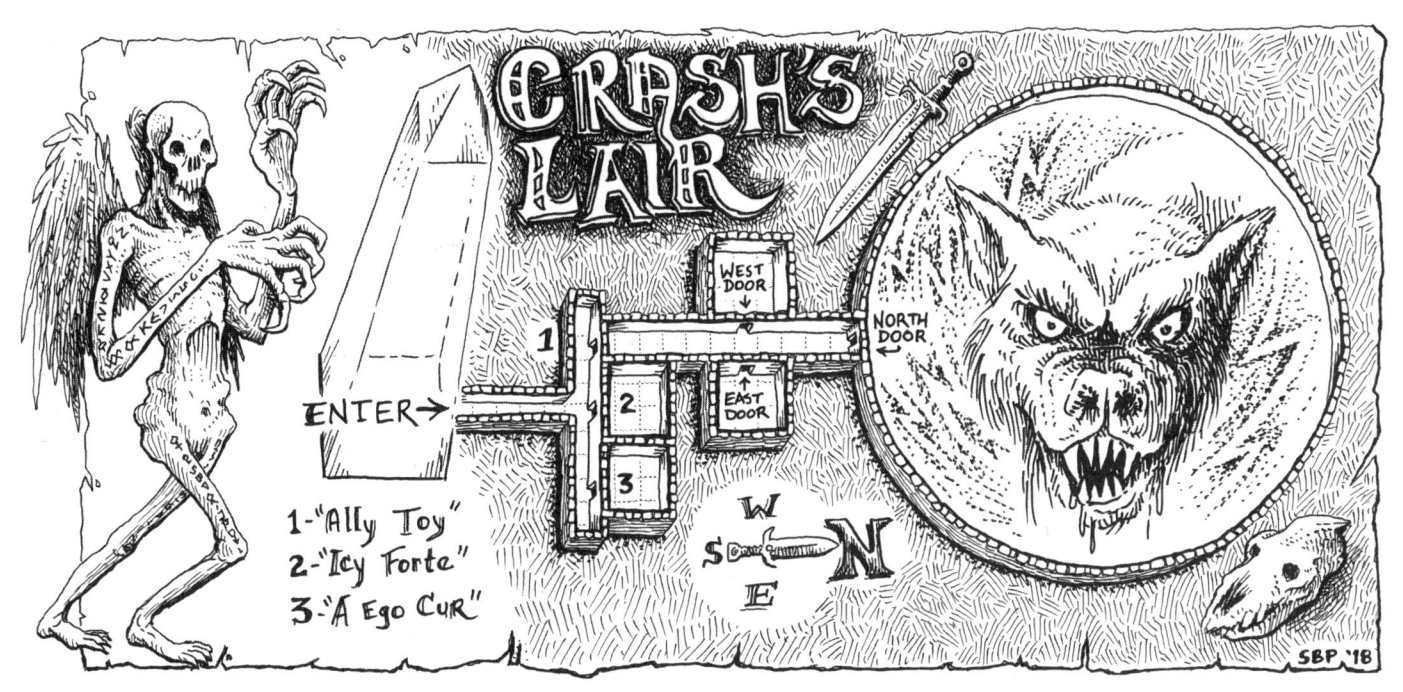

1 - "Ally Toy"
2 - "Icy Forte"
3 - "A Ego Cur"

Carved upon the Ghoul Angel's chest in sharp relief there is the following dedication:

Since our bond, in the Astral Mists,

After I freed you from the cursed Guild of Numismatists

You've been courageous even in darkest night,

As great as any heroic knight

In our battles few could compare,

To the great ferocity you always laid bare

And your loyalty was such a great treasure

T'was worth more beyond any measure,

So dear Crash never give up chase,

Until I find a cure, it's your only grace

After dispatching the Ghoul Angel the PCs may pass through north, down a 40' long tunnel that ends in a hallway with three doors. The doors are locked (DC 15 pick locks), and 10' tall and wide. They look similar except for the unique words written on each. These are anagrams of Crash's three attributes noted in the dedication on the Ghoul Angel: Courage, Ferocity, and Loyalty. The first door leads to Crash's lair, as loyalty is the most important attribute, as noted in the dedication. The anagram on the first door also provides a clue how to get Crash's attention in the final room. The other two are trapped, as detailed below. (If the PCs decide to hack through the doors their weapons will rebound against them, as the doors are made of a rubber like substance.) Only acid or cold energy can damage the doors. All doors in the lair have 50 hit points. Note: the doors are magically obscured that any are trapped.

Door 1: "Ally Toy": Beyond this door there is a hallway that leads to Crash's lair.

Door 2: "Icy Forte": Opening this door will reveal the statue of a white dragon head, which immediately breathes a freezing wind that does 51 points of damage. A successful DC 19 Fortitude save will result in half damage. A saving throw roll of a 1 indicates a pc is killed instantly and frozen solid. If the door isn't closed, the dragon will breathe again every two rounds.

Door 3: "A Ego Cur": Opening this door will reveal a wall covered in several evil looking dog skulls with their brains exposed. These are glistening and pulsating and connected together by gold wires organized in a way to make the entire assembly look like one giant dog skull. This alchemic horror will instantly attack as soon as the door is opened, releasing a mind blast that causes 6d6 damage. A successful DC 19 Willpower save will negate this effect, but even if successful the PCs effected will be stunned for 1d4 rounds. Note a saving throw roll of a 1 will result in death, as the mental blast has turned the PC's mind into goo. If the door is left open, the brains will attack the PCs every two rounds.

Beyond the first door there is a 100-foot-long hallway that leads north, and ends in a door. At fifty feet there is also a door to the east and west side of the hallway.

The East Door: The door to this room is locked (DC 15 pick locks to unlock). The room beyond has many of Crash's favorite things, including a food bowl made of ivory, a three-foot diameter ball, a 20' by 10' blanket, and a barrel full of 7-foot-long bones. There is also a gold leash, 50' long. The leash is disguised by a powerful illusion. In reality it is a cursed rope that when shown to Crash will cause him to attack the bearer immediately.

The West Door: The west door isn't locked. Inside there are numerous trophies and statutes that represent the many foes defeated by Crash. These include a Chaos Knight, a giant cat with three heads, and many more unusual creatures. There are 2d30 objects here with a value of 4d4x100 gold pieces each. Note these items are exceptionally awkward to carry and often quite heavy.

The North Door: Beyond this locked door (DC 15 pick locks to unlock) there is a 200' diameter round room covered in short blue grass. Crash is seen running around in a circle at the outer perimeter of the room chasing a silver rabbit.

Crash is a 15' tall hound with close cropped white fur and crystal blue eyes. Electricity courses across and around his body endlessly. Crash is a muscular and beautiful hound despite his several scars. He moves 50' a round. The rabbit is 5' tall, and made of silver and has two large teeth. If Crash stops chasing it, the rabbit will stop and attempt to bait the hound to make it chase it again. The rabbit moves 60' a round.

Yonaxis put Crash is in the lair to forestall a dreaded curse – which causes the hound to age whenever he stops moving. The enchanted rabbit was also created by the mage – which causes Crash to chase it without surcease. The grass in the room both renews the hound's fatigue and releases an essence that provides sustenance, which prevents the hound from collapsing from exhaustion.

The only way to get Crash's attention and stop chasing the rabbit is to present him the ball from the previous room. After obtaining Crash's attention, and once the PCs provide the Snass' message, the hound will bolt down the hallway and jump into the Astral Mists to aid its master.

Crash the Astral Hound: Init +8; Atk bite +10 melee (1d8+4), claw +10 melee (1d12+40), or crash +10 melee (3d12+4); AC 20; HD 8d12; hp 56; MV 50'; ACT 4d20; SP can see and travel into the Astral Plane at will, regeneration (1d8 hp/round); SV Fort +10, Ref +8, Will +8; AL L.

Day 3 Encounter A – One Eye Morty: One Eye Morty is an insane, homeless picker, who visits the tower monthly to sell the things he's found in Naos. He is a boisterous salesman. He shares that he is saving money to buy a new eye. He offers to sell the whole lot for 600 gold! If pressed, he sells the items individually and prices based on the difficulty of obtaining them. Prices are as below:

- 5' tall candle made with pieces of fine jade, 100 sp.
- Foldable bucket made of shark hide, 15 gp.
- Giant Mithril fish hook with 200' of silk twine, 200 gp.
- Ladies boot with gold buckle, covered in small jewels (with a severed woman's foot inside), 100 gp.
- Seaweed necklace with pearls (completely covered in dried blood), 200 gp.
- A perfectly smooth black branch without bark and several short limbs. This is a living Elder Sign Branch. The branch provides constant Protection from Evil to the wielder and can be used in combat as a +2 trident versus evil beings (1d8+2). The branch also does double damage to demons. The branch will communicate its purpose empathically to the holder, when facing such opponent. 150 gp.

Morty found these items under the docks at the outskirts of the city. He has no idea of the true nature or purpose of these items or their real value.

NPC Profile: One Eye Morty is crazy and half-blind, but has a sage level knowledge of weather, fishing and moonshine. He wears rags, an eye patch, and a dead parrot on his shoulder. Despite his obvious state of squalor Morty is strangely exceptionally lucky in finding treasure among trash.

One Eye Morty: Init -2; Atk punch -2 melee (1); AC 9; HD 1d8; hp 4; MV 30'; Act 1d20; SV Fort -2, Ref -2, Will +2; AL C. Equipment: A bag of trash.

Morty has a base 75% chance of knowing the answer to any question regarding weather, fishing or moonshine. Very easy questions are 10-20% more likely to be known, while difficult questions are 10-20% less likely to be known.

Day 3 Encounter B – Cursed Nirb: A magical portal appears in front of the tower and Nirb, a swamp trapper, runs out yelling "Help!" He is filthy, and wearing torn clothing.

Nirb runs to a random character and immediately spits out two bog frogs, which will gain a free surprise attack. On the following rounds, Nirb spits out another frog at initiative counts 15, 7 and 3. Immediately after they are spit out the frogs grow giant sized and attack whichever PC is closest to them.

There is also frog demon in Nirb's stomach spawning the frogs that needs to be cut out or exorcised to stop Nirb from spewing the amphibians. A remove curse spell cast on Nirb will also fix the problem. If a Paralyzation spell is successfully cast on Nirb he will stop spitting frogs – but the act will also cause Nirb to die, explosively.

Giant Bog Frogs (5 or more): Init +1; Atk tongue +2 melee (stuck then swallowed), bite +2 melee (1d6+1), or claws +2 (1d4+1); AC 14; HD 3d6; hp 9 each; MV 20' or swim 10'; Act 3d20; SP stuck (DC 14 Ref save or be stuck and swallowed in 1d4 rounds); SV Fort +2, Ref +1, Will +0; AL N.

The giant bog frogs will initiate with their tongue attack. If the tongue attack fails the frog will bite the following round. Targets struck and stuck by the tongue will be swallowed in 1d4 rounds. An attack roll of a natural 20 also means the target is swallowed

Page 12

VOKUF GREENVEIN SUFFERS BATRACIAN CORRUPTION!

immediately. Once swallowed, victims are at -4 to all attacks, due the confined nature of being trapped in the frog's gullet. Swallowed victims can escape after causing 2 points of damage, which first requires an attack roll of 18. If the target doesn't escape in three rounds, the victim dies.

If Nirb dies, a small red frog crawls out of his guts, and then grows into a 15' long Frog Demon and attacks.

Frog Demon (type I demon, Bobugbubilz): Init +2; Atk tongue +4 melee (stuck then swallowed) or bite +6 melee (1d8+2); AC 13; HD 4d12; hp 24; MV 20' or swim 10'; Act 1d20; SP demon traits, stuck (DC 16 Ref save or be stuck and swallowed in 1d4 rounds); SV Fort +4, Ref +2, Will +0; AL C.

The frog demon with initiate with its attack as the giant bog frogs above.

Nirb: Init +2; Atk fist +2 melee (1d3+1) AC 15; HD 3d8; hp 12; MV 20'; Act 1d20; SV Fort+2, Ref +2, Will +0; AL C.

NPC Profile: Nirb is a hungry and poor trapper who foolishly ventured onto the lands of Horrible the Witch, to look for game, and tried to steal one of her goats. If asked, he describes the witch as a beautiful, tall woman with perfect skin, red hair, and black eyes. Also if he survives the encounter Nirb will gladly become the PCs' henchman.

Day 3 Encounter C – Reaper Arrives: A masked man (a Reaper) wearing a pointy red hood and a black feathered cloak arrives riding a very large grey bird (a Reaper's Minion). The black bird has a gray featherless head, a long razor-sharp beak that seems to smile, and large talons. The bird yells "5, 5, 5, 5" over and over until it lands. The number 5 been painted on its left and right side of its body.

As soon as the bird lands on the perch on the tower grounds (area 8) the Reaper jumps off, floating to the ground and approaches the PC with the highest personality score. After handing the PC a note (see Handout B) he will return to his mount and fly away.

Reaper: Init +5; Atk longsword +6 melee (1d8+3) or whip +7 missile fire (1d3+1d6 lightning+shock); AC 17; HD 5d8; hp 20; MV 20'; Act 2d20; SP shock (DC 15 Fort save or be stunned 1d4 rounds); SV Fort +4, Ref +4, Will +2; AL C.

Reaper's Minion: Init +2; Atk beak +4 melee (5d8); AC 15; HD 10d8; hp 40; MV fly 50'; Act 3d20; SV Fort +4, Ref +3, Will +3; AL L.

Night 3 Encounter A – Aspect of Cthulhu: (Optional: If the party didn't buy the Elder Sign Branch from Morty, then roll on the Random Die Drop Encounter Generator on page 23 or perhaps have Nigella cause additional problems for the PCs if she has been previously encountered.)

A group of peasants (actually cultists) walk up the path to the tower and demands return of the branch, which they claim was stolen. These are servants of Cthulhu, an Aspect of Cthulhu is hidden among them disguised as a peasant! If the PCs refuse, they will attack. If the Aspect of Cthulhu loses 50% of its hit points it will flee, via teleport.

Cultists (10): Init +1; Atk pitchfork +1 melee (1d8+1); AC 14; HD 2d4; hp 5 each; MV 30'; Act 1d20; SV Fort +2, Ref -1, Will +1; AL C.

Aspect of Cthulhu: Init +3; Atk tentacle +8 melee (2d4) or mind scythe sphere +8 missile fire (4d10+paralyzed); AC 18; HD 8d10; hp 66; MV 20', fly 20' swim 40'; Act special; SP 4 tentacles (4 successful tentacles attacks cause death in 1d4 rounds), 1 mind scythe attack per round (paralyzed for 1d4 rounds, DC 18 Will save for half damage, range 20' radius), can teleport at will; SV Fort +8, Ref +5, Will +9; AL C.

Day 4 Encounter A – DARE Arrives: A wood golem walks forward. He has four gems across his chest–a diamond, amethyst, ruby and emerald. He first says, "My name is DARE, and I don't want to be here…" He continues with similar statements such as "I traveled a short distance to get here" or "I made good friends with the redcaps outside the city. They were so nice" and "I don't want to be here!" He repeats variations of the above and answers any question with the exact opposite of the truth. He ends his statements with "My name is Dare," which should help clue the PCs on the nature of his plight. DARE's real name is Erad.

Erad was was sent to the tower to deliver a gift on behalf of his mistress, the Lady Esmeralda. He encountered a group of redcap fey – who reversed the order of the gems on his chest – which caused his malfunction. In addition, the fey put a "kick me sign" on his back, drew womanly lips on his face and glued hay on his head to resemble hair.

If the PCs replace the gems on his chest, in reverse order, to reflect his true name, (E)merald (R)uby (A)methyst (D)iamond, the golem will be fixed and be able to speak truthfully. If two gems are misplaced, he attacks. After the players fix the golem, he will say "Thank you, I am Erad!" and then opens a hidden cabinet in his chest and hands over a note and a tree sapling (see Handout C).

Page 14

The sapling is a Sparkle Tree with small Fey who live within it. If planted, the tree grows rapidly and soft, beautiful singing can be heard. The tree has a beautiful soft glow with sparkles that appear randomly across its leaves and branches. Anyone who sleeps under the tree heals 3 points of damage a night and has pleasant dreams.

DARE (Erad) the Wood Golem: Init: +1; Atk fist +5 melee (1d10+3); AC 14; HD 6d8; hp 38; MV 20'; Act 2d20; SP double damage from fire; SV Fort +8, Ref +2, Will +4; AL L.

Day 4 Encounter B – Delivering the Prisoner Xoxoz the Malevolent: A Reaper arrives on it's bird (this time painted with a 7 on its side, screeching, "7, 7, 7," over and over until it lands), dragging behind a weightless cube of darkness on a long chain. The Reaper's rider gives the chain to the PCs and leaves. The Reaper has brought Xoxoz the Malevolent–the Daemon Fiend.

If the PCs drag the chain the Minotaur Door, it will open, and the two statues in front will animate, take the chain and enter beyond. The doors will close the moment they do so. Note those who look inside must make a DC 18 Fortitude save or be paralyzed for 1d4 rounds. Beyond the door is a bridge that leads to an inter-dimensional prison, in the form of a mazed-covered cube.

Night 4 Encounter A – Wickstrom the Chandler: Wickstrom is an ancient vampire dressed in fine robes, wearing two large candles on his shoulders and walks with a staff topped with a candle. He is wearing a device that makes it impossible to detect his alignment (Chaotic).

He brings the Candles of Myrrh, and he expects to be paid 1,000 gp plus a small jug (1 liter) of human blood. When given the jar, he opens and tastes it to ensure its quality. Unfortunately, the blood does not meet the vampire's standards–and he demands more or different blood–preferably from a virgin. He will draw the blood with a sharp nail from any who volunteer (which will cause only 1 hp of damage). Conversely he will demand 1,000 gp if the PCs won't replace the blood.

The PCs should bring the candles to the Wizard Door. When they do, it will open revealing several gnome golems made of glass, organizing and preparing ingredients, and making potions. They will stop this work shortly after the door opens, come out and take the candles. The door will close immediately after they return inside.

After the door closes, the area above the Wizard's Door suddenly glows with golden light, and then it quickly travels up the tower and becomes a beam of light that pierces the sky. After the beam appears it connects with the other two beams and forms a triangle. The sky within the triangle starts to slowly churn.

Wickstrom the Ancient Vampire Chandler: Init: +6; Atk bite +10 melee (2d6+enthralled), claws +10 melee (1d8+drain); AC 16; HD 14d8; hp 66; MV 30', fly 40'; Act 3d24; SP enthralled, Strength drain, incorporeal at will, immune to non-magical weapons, un-dead traits; SV Fort +4, Ref+6, Will +4; AL C. Equipment: Candle topped staff, coin purse with 200 gp, a nail file, tinder box, five candles. Necklace of Obfuscation; SP Obscures the alignment of the wearer.

Any creature bitten by an ancient vampire may become a vampire spawn (DC 14 Fortitude save to resist). Vampire spawn are thralls; they will do whatever their master requires. Beyond causing damage, each claw attack from an ancient vampire temporarily drains its victim of 1d6 Strength points.

Vampires are un-dead, and thus can be turned by clerics. They feed on blood, and are immune to critical hits, disease, and poison. As un-dead, they are immune to sleep, charm, and paralysis spells, as well as other mental effects and cold damage. In addition, they take 1d20 damage a round when exposed to either sunlight or moving water.

Attacks against a vampire with a sharpened wooden stake (1d4) have a crit range of 16-20; such results are rolled on Crit Table V on page 86 of the DCC RPG rule book.

NPC Profile: Wickstrom is an ancient vampire, and has no ambition beyond making exquisite candles. He speaks slowly with exceptional etiquette, which hints at his history of wealth and privilege.

Night 4 Encounter B – Breakout!: Two teams (hatches) of eight fell elves work together to free Xoxoz. Their goal is to ultimately break down the Dragon Door, and destroy Yonaxis or at least prevent him from casting his spell.

The first team with the captain, lieutenant, and guards will attack the PCs directly in front of the tower. Unless the PCs take precautions, they should get a free round to attack the PCs. When Team 1 begins their attack the second team will enter the estate near the cottage and move quickly to the Minotaur Door. It will take Team 2 eight rounds to cross the wall and moat, open the Minotaur door, and summon Xoxoz (using a scroll). The fell elves cross the wall and moat using potions of flying. (To prepare for the attack the fell elves consulted a sage, and learned the secret as to how to open the tower's doors.) After they free Xoxoz their next move will be to open the Dragon Door and attack Yonaxis!

Page 15

TEAM 1

Fell Elf Hatch Lieutenant: Init +1; Atk longsword +3 melee (1d8) or crossbow +3 missile fire (1d6+poison); AC 15; HD 4d8; hp 17; MV 25'; Act 1d20; SP poison (DC 15 Fort save or slept in 1d4 rounds for 1d4 rounds), immune to charm and sleep spells, infravision, conjure sphere of darkness (1' radius) once per day, shoots webbing 5' x 5' from its fingers 1 a day (+3 missile fire, target stuck for 2d4 rounds, unless DC 18 Strength check is made), vulnerable to sunlight (suffers 1d4 damage per round in sunlight and -1d on all rolls from the sun and magical light); SV Fort +1, Ref +2, Will +2; AL C.

The lieutenant wears +1 mithril chainmail (but alas has a poor Agility) and wields a longsword and crossbow made of the same material.

Fell Elf Captain: Init +2; Atk longsword +2 melee (1d8) or crossbow +3 missile fire (1d6+poison); AC 17; HD 3d8; hp 21; Act 1d20; MV 25'; SP poison (DC 15 Fort save or slept in 1d4 rounds for 1d4 rounds), immune to charm and sleep spells, infravision, conjure sphere of darkness (1' radius) once per day, vulnerable to sunlight (suffers 1d4 damage per round in sunlight and -1d on all rolls from the sun and magical light); SV Fort +2, Ref +3, Will +2; AL C.

The captain wears mithril chainmail and wields a longsword and crossbow made of the same material.

Fell Elf Warriors (6): Init +1; Atk longsword +1 melee (1d8) or crossbow +2 (1d6 + poison); AC 13; HD 2d8; hp 9 each; MV 25'; SP poison (DC 15 Fort save or fall asleep in 1d4 rounds for 1d4 rounds), immune to charm and sleep spells, infravision, vulnerable to sunlight (suffers 1d4 damage per round in sunlight and -1d on all rolls from the sun and magical light); SV Fort +1, Ref +2, Will +1; AL C.

These elves wield mithril longswords and crossbows. They wear a patchwork of obviously slapdash and mismatched leather and mithril pieces.

TEAM 2

Fell Elf Hatch Mistress: Init +3; Atk two-handed sword +5 melee (1d10+2) or dagger +5 melee (1d4); AC 17; HD 4d8; hp 21; Act 1d20+1d14; MV 25'; SP immune to charm and sleep spells, infravision, conjure sphere of darkness (1' radius) once per day, shoot webbing 5' x 5' from its fingers 1 a day (+3 missile, target stuck for 2d4 rounds, unless a DC 18 Strength check is made), polymorph into a giant spider* once a day, vulnerable to sunlight (suffers 1d4 damage per round in sunlight and -1d on all rolls from the sun and magical light); SV Fort +5, Ref +3, Will +2; AL C.

The Mistress is the leader of the squad of fell elves. She wears +1 mithril chainmail and wields a +1 two-handed sword (due to exceptional craftsmanship) and a dagger made of the same material. While wielding the two-handed sword a 1d16 is used to roll for initiative.

*Hatch Mistress in Giant Fell Spider Form: Init +3; Atk bite +8 melee (1d10+2+poison); AC 16; HD 4d10; hp 22; MV 50' or climb 50'; Act 3d20; SP poison (DC 15 Fort save or death in 1d4 rounds), vulnerable to sunlight (suffers 1d4 damage per round in sunlight and -1d on all rolls from the sun and magical light), casts web (per spell) once per day (+5 spell check); SV Fort +9, Ref +4, Will -2; AL C.

Fell spiders are smoky grey in color, covered in small black dots. Their many malevolent eyes are milky white, while their jagged and poisonous mandibles are black.

Fell Elf Captain: Init +2; Atk longsword +2 melee (1d8) or crossbow +3 missile fire (1d6+poison); AC 17; HD 3d8; hp 21; MV 25'; Act 1d20; SP poison (DC 15 Fort save or fall asleep in 1d4 rounds for 1d4 rounds), immune to charm and sleep spells, conjure sphere of darkness (1' radius) once per day, vulnerable to sunlight (suffers 1d4 damage per round in sunlight and -1d on all rolls from the sun and magical light); SV Fort +2, Ref +3, Will +2; AL C.

The captain wears mithril chainmail and wields a longsword and crossbow made of the same material.

Fell Elf Warriors (5): Init +1; Atk longsword +1 melee (1d8) or crossbow +2 missile fire (1d6+poison); AC 13; HD 2d8; hp 9 each; MV 25'; AC 13; SP poison (DC 15 Fort save or slept in 1d4 rounds for 1d4 rounds), immune to charm and sleep spells, infravision, vulnerable to sunlight (suffers 1d4 damage per round in sunlight and -1d on all rolls from the sun and magical light); SV Fort +1, Ref +2, Will +1; AL C.

The elves wield mithril longswords and crossbows. They wear a patchwork of leather and mithril pieces.

Fell elves are 5' tall, and have chalky dark grey skin, black eyes and hair. Both males and females wear their spiky hair down to their waists. Within their well groomed and bejeweled hair they also store small crystalized bones of their enemies. The fell elves' faces are misshapen and their skin is pitted. Once beautiful, their form became corrupted after living below the earth, among its alien fungi for several millennia.

Note: Fell elves will typically start an attack using their crossbows. These two-handed weapons require the use of a 1d16 when rolling initiative for this initial attack. Also, it may be possible the PCs see the second team of fell elves moving toward the Minotaur door – especially if they've planted the Sparkle Tree (from Erad/ DARE) next to the Weskeebs Tree, which will illuminate the west side of the tower in soft light. After two rounds of combat with the first group of fell elves, allow the PCs a DC 20 Intelligence check (+3 if the Sparkle Tree was planted) to determine whether they notice the second group advancing towards the Minotaur door.

Xoxoz the Malevolent–the Daemon Fiend: Init +3; Atk claws +10 melee (1d10), maw +10 melee (3d6) or eye attack +10 missile fire (varies, see below); AC varies (see hit locations below); HD 11d12; hp varies (see hit locations below); Act 5d20; MV 5', using two arms 15', using four arms 30'; SP grab, maw bite, acid snouts, magic resistance 50%, immune to charm and sleep spells; SV Fort +9, Ref +2, Will +1; AL C.

Xoxoz is seven feet tall monstrosity with five arms, each with three clawed fingers. Upon the palm of each hand is a large eye. Its mouth is full of teeth and vertically bisects the top portion of the creature. The body of the creature is covered in small snouts. It has no legs – rather a single thick stalk, with multiple toes covered in think nails.

As its basic attack, the creature uses two hands to pick up a creature and put it in its maw. Two successful claw attacks grabs a creature, escape requires a successful mighty deed or a DC 18 Strength check. In the following round, grabbed creatures will be lifted above the creature so it can be eaten with a bite attack

Xoxoz Eye Attacks

d6	Result
1	Psionic Razor eye
2	Color Spray eye*
3	Luck Eater eye
5	Magic Missile eye*
6	Paralyzation eye

*See the spell noted in the DCC RPG rulebook. Spellchecks made at +10.

Xoxoz Hit Location

d100	Result
1	Psionic Razor eye†
2	Color Spray eye†
3	Luck Eater eye†
5	Magic Missile eye†
6	Paralyzation eye†
7-30	**Arm (AC 18, hp 10 each):** Roll 1d5 to determine which arm by its associated eye is hit: (1) Psionic razor eye, (2) Color Spray eye, (3) Luck Eater, (4) Magic Missile eye, or (6) Paralyzation eye. Destroying an arm also destroys its associated eyeball.
31-00	Body (AC 15, hp 55)††

†Destroying an eyeball only destroys its associated attack.

††Destroying the body will kill the creature and cause it to explode, causing 4d6 acid damage to everyone with 10' of the creature (DC 15 Ref save for half). Also, if Xoxoz is killed, any Luck stolen from the party is returned, plus 1 more for each PC who engaged it in combat.

(1 per round) for 3d6 damage. Note, a roll of 18-20 indicates the trapped being is swallowed. Swallowed creatures take 3d6 damage a round, attacks from within are made at -5 due to the constricting nature of the gullet. Swallowed PCs who cause 10 points of damage will be spit out; such victims that fail to escape the beast's gullet in three rounds die. While trying to eat a PC, the other three arms are used to position the eyes to attack the other party members.

While in melee, Xoxoz releases acid through the snouts covering his body, which cause 4d6 damage to those in a 3' radius (DC 18 Fort save for half damage). Those who fail their save also take 1d4 damage for the following 1d4 rounds. Finally, anyone hit by this acid must make a saving throw for their armor and shields.

Eye attacks: For each eye attack roll a 1d6 to indicate the spell effect for each attack: (1) Psionic Razor (one target, range 30 yards, 3d6 damage), (2) Color Spray*, (3) Luck Eater (target loses 1d4 Luck), (4) magic missile (), or (5) Paralyzation (one target, range 30 yards, DC 18 Will save or paralyzed for 1d6 rounds).

When the Xoxoz is hit, roll on the Xocoz Hit Location Table. The AC and hit points are noted for each location as well. Hit location (roll 1d100).

Day 5 – Yonaxis Summons the Fesprul: At dawn Yonaxis teleports the PCs to the top of the tower and summons the creature. With arms casting and weaving the sky above the tower within the triangle of light swirls and becomes purple and green. With arms weaving he causes the beams of light and triangle to spin.

If available, he grabs the Elder Sign from the PCs, and throws it into the triangle and pierces the sky, ripping a hole. (Without the Elder Sign branch, Yonaxis will magically extend his arm, doing the same thing.)

With the triangle spinning Yonaxis claps his hands above his head, and moves his hands skyward in a grasping motion. From the hole within the triangle the face of a large wasp with a mouth full of tentacles appears and wiggles his head through the opening.

The creature summoned is a Fesprul, the fabled "Devourer of Gates." If the daemon fails its saving throw (see below) it pulls its head out and then sticks its abdomen through the hole in the sky, and secretes a massive (50' wide) egg covered in gold. The creature then leaves.

The egg falls from the sky like a meteor, strikes the ground with a loud crash and immediately cracks open. From the cracked egg, a spawn crawls forth. The creature is 100' long with dozens of wings, a body that is dark red and striped black with hundreds of clawed feelers and the head of a wasp full of tentacles. After emerging from the egg, the Fesprul's spawn bows down to Yonaxis. Now under its control, Yonaxis speaks to the creature in an arcane tongue and then points to the sky. The spawn then jumps to fly and begins its servitude. However, if the Fesprul makes its saving throw, it attacks the party. If the creature is reduced to 50% hit points it will flee back through the hole in the sky, from whence it came.

The Fesprul is a 10 HD daemon. It must make a Willpower save against Yonaxis's spell check (1d20+13). However, for every item acquired noted below, the DC increases by 2 points (or a maximum of 8 points total).

- Wickstrom's Candles
- Bronze Anvil (or only +1 bonus if the Dwarven Anvil is used)
- Honeycakes
- Elder Sign Branch

Thus if all the items are gathered, the Fesprul's DC to break the binding will be increased by +8. Note: the creature does not get magic resistance against the summoning because its True Name was used in casting the spell.

If the binding spell fails, roll initiative. Below is a summary of the tactics used if battle should occur.

Fesprul (type IV demon): Init +4; Atk tentacle melee +12 melee (4d6+6) and stunning eye +12 missile fire (stun); AC 21; HD 15d12; hp 90; MV 40" or fly 60"; Act 11d20; SP stun (DC 22 Fort save to resist), swallow whole, spells (check +8, detect good, scare), demon traits, 30% magic resistant; SV Fort +12, Ref +0, Will +10; AL C.

Page 17

The Fesprul is a gargantuan (200' long) red wasp with a mouth filled with ten 100' long yellow tentacles that end in a sharp stinger. The being has multiple sets of wings that are black and yellow. Its eyes scintillate between red, yellow, and orange.

When attacking, the Fesprul thrusts its head and upper torso out of a hole in the sky. While in the hole its AC is 17 due to its limited mobility. When it starts its attack, it buzzes its wings generating a significant wind; any PC trying to engage it in melee must make a DC 15 Strength check to approach it and to keep engaging it every round. Beyond this, it focuses its eye attack on one target (DC 22 Fortitude save or be stunned 1d5 rounds) and then uses its ten 100' tentacles to attack its foes. The Fesprul crits on a 17-20. In addition to its demon critical effect, the following round the target may get swallowed (DC 22 Strength check to break free). Swallowed creatures take 4d6+6 damage until freed.

Yonaxis the Magnificent (10th level wizard): Init +1; Atk dagger "Glosnog" +4 melee (1d4+4) or wizard staff +5 melee (1d4+11); AC 13; HD 10d4; hp 63; MV 30" or fly 60"; Act 2d20+1d14; SP spells (see below); SV Fort +9, Ref +8, Will +5; AL N.

Spells (check +13):
Level 1: Color Spray, Comprehend Languages, Mending, Invoke Patron (The King of Elfland), Patron Bond (The King of Elfland)

Level 2: Levitate, Scorching Ray, Wizard's Staff

Level 3: Breathe Life, Lightning, The Dreaming

Level 4: Control Fire, Control Ice, Polymorph, Transmutatio

Level 5: Hepsoj's Fecund Fungi, Replication

Yonaxis is a wizened and charismatic mage who has a perfectly groomed mustache and short pointy grey beard. He wears blue robes and a skullcap with two ram horns. He wields a magic dagger, called Glosnog, which enables flight to 3d4 individuals, and allows him to communicate to any of his minions, and teleport any of them to him as well.

Yonaxis created a wizard's staff (using the spell of the same name). This is a +1 weapon, which inflicts 1d4+11 when a successful hit is scored against a foe. The staff also emits light in a 20' radius, which can be turned on or off and vary in intensity from candlelight to full daylight, at the caster's discretion. The staff provides +2 to spell checks when Yonaxis casts control fire, control ice, and polymorph. Finally, the staff also grants a +2 bonus to the wizard's saving throws and armor class.

Sorshine the Head Apprentice (5th level wizard): Init +0; Atk staff +2 melee (1d4); AC 11; HD 5d4; hp 16; MV 30'; Act 1d20+1d14; SP spells; SV Fort +2, Ref +1, Will +3; AL L.

Spells (check +7):

Level 1: Magic Missile, Ropework, Sleep

Level 2: Fireball, Monster Summoning, Scorching Ray

Level 3: Dispel Magic, Haste

Snass the Lesser Apprentice (3rd level wizard): Init +0; Atk staff +2 melee (1d4); AC 11; HD 3d4; hp 12; MV 30'; Act 1d20; SP spells; SV Fort +1, Ref +1, Will +3; AL N.

Spells (check +6):

Level 1: Choking Cloud, Color Spray, Enlarge, Magic Missile-

Level 2: Scorching Ray

Tactics that Yonaxis, Sorshine, and Snass use against the Fesprul:

Round 1. If Yonaxis fails to bind the Fesprul, his first action is to cast banish (the cleric spell, modified for mage use) from a scroll. Sorshine will cast dispel magic, in attempt to close the gate which brought the creature, with the hope it will prevent it from entering Naos, uncontrolled. To be successful, both wizards must overcome the Fesprul's magic resistance (31 or higher must be rolled on 1d100). If magic resistance is overcome, the gate closes in 2d4 rounds. Snass will cower, but encourage the PCs to fight it, with very specific tactics.

Round 2. If the Fesprul is successful a second time resisting the spell, Yonaxis invokes patron and spellburns 7 points to improve his roll. Sorshine will attempt another dispel magic. Snass will continue to cower and offer encouragement.

Round 3. If all else fails, the wizards will fight with all of their considerable abilities.

THE END

If Yonaxis is successful in binding the Spawn, he rewards each player with a valuable gem (2,000 gp), and the promise to enchant one weapon, plus an offer to become Champions of the Tower. This title will provide the PCs a permanent residence on Yonaxis' estate and social status slightly less than that of nobility. If the PCs decline the offer, the mage will teleport the PCs back home.

If Yonaxis is not successful in his quest, he will give each surviving character a gem valued at 1,000 gp and then send them back home.

THE RANDOM DIE DROP ENCOUNTER GENERATOR

An optional die drop table is included in this module to increase the complexity and number of encounters in the adventure. It can be used two different ways. First, prior to each encounter (as noted in the outline on page 2) roll 1d20 on the die drop table below. The resulting NPC will engage the player characters during the encounter. Even numbers indicate the being will positively advise or influence the interaction in the respective encounter. Odd numbers, on the other hand, means a more negative influence during the encounter. Also the higher the number rolled the more substantial the tower denizen will become: (1-10) only the NPC's voice will be heard, (11-15) indicates the being's face will appear on the tower (and no others on the tower at that time) and (16-20) means the being will physically appear in ghostly form and interact with the characters during the encounter. Profiles for these beings are provided to aid the judge when role playing the encounters.

The second use of the random die drop table is to generate additional encounters, whenever desired. In playtests the table was used whenever the players rolled a 20 or 1 in a combat. As noted in the overview above, even and odd numbers should influence how the tower denizen will interact with the PCs. For example, a die drop result "11. Efreet Female" is normally an encounter that results in the PCs being attacked. In one playtest a 20 was rolled on the Efreet illustration – which indicated the encounter should be extremely positive. In that instance the judge determined the Efreet appeared in the skies above (as normal) but instead of attacking, she cried and her raining tears became rubies when they hit the ground. (2d6 gems worth 100 gp each).

Beyond the mechanics noted, PCs also have an option of altering the drop die roll – by burning Luck to change the results. Burning Luck can either alter the die result (up or down) or force a second role on the table. Due to the unusual nature of the tower a minimum of 5 Luck points must be burned to move a die result up or down one point. However, to re-roll a result on the table requires only burning one Luck point. These mechanics should be shared with the players prior to play (see table on page 23).

THE RANDOM DIE DROP ENCOUNTER RESULTS

1. The Flesh Tailor: A grotesque, young man with sagging skin and a wandering left eye comes onto the grounds to sell his wares–robes made from flesh from various humanoids. His name is Sanguine and he speaks with a lisp. His robes are well made. He charges 100 gp per robe (he has several available).

Sanguine: Init -1; Atk club +1 melee (1d4) AC 11; HD 1d8; hp 5; MV 30'; Act 1d20; SV Fort +1, Ref +0, Will +2; AL N.

NPC Profile: Cheerful, with unusual interest in skin, the imprisoned old man's obsession has encouraged others to collect and experiment with skins.

2. Orc Queen: A group of large pigs runs onto the estate. They wander around, looking for things to eat. Some try to drink from the moat while others touch the tower and get burned to death.

NPC Profile: The image of the orc queen yells rudely at the PCs from the tower, but will speak sweetly to the pigs that wander onto the estate.

Wild Pig (3d6): Init +1; Atk gore +2 melee (1d4); AC 12; HD 1d6; hp 3 each; MV 20'; Act 1d20; SV Fort +3, Ref +1, Will +0; AL CN.

3. The Dwarf Berserker: Mad whispers from the dwarf image on the tower are spoken for 3 rounds. The whispers warn of an invasion of trolls and the image demands freedom. After 1 turn, 2d4 trolls charge the tower. When the trolls appear, the dwarf will likewise manifest, aiding the party in fighting them.

Troll (2d4): Init +6; Atk bite +10 melee (2d8+6) or claw +8 melee (2d6); AC 19; HD 8d8+6; hp 38 each; MV 40'; Act 3d20; SP stench, regeneration, immune to critical hits, immune to mind-affecting spells, vulnerable to fire; SV Fort +10, Ref +5, Will +8; AL C.

Dwarf Berserker: Init -1; Atk battleaxe +2+1d7(deed) melee (1d10+2+deed roll); AC 14; HD 5d10; hp 27; MV 20'; Act 1d20+1d14; SP mighty deeds (d7), shield bash (make an extra 1d14 attack with your shield, 1d3 damage); Fort +2, Ref +1, Will +1; AL N.

NPC Profile: Insane and obsessed with killing trolls. He is fated to fight trolls, and they him, until the end of time.

4. Bliss the Dreaded Serpent Sorcerer: Any wizard PCs in the group will be offered power if they help the imprisoned sorcerer. If a PC agrees, he will be possessed (no save) by Bliss. The sorcerer merely wants revenge, and will work subtly to isolate and murder each guardian of the tower, and then will attempt to destroy Yonaxis.

NPC Profile: Charismatic, sly, and evil to its core. It's only goal is to cause chaos.

If Bliss possesses a PC, it will assume their physical attributes. Bliss's Intelligence, Wisdom and Charisma are all 16. Once freed, Bliss can use its spellcasting abilities as an 8th-level wizard; its spell check is d20+12. Remaining memorized spells are noted below:

Level 1: Enlarge, Mending, Read Magic, Runic Alphabet, Sleep, Ventriloquism

Level 2: Levitate

Level 3: Demon Summoning, Planar Step

Level 4: Control Ice

5. Anabella the Young Vampire: An old man named Maurice comes to the tower to speak to Anabella. He was her first love before she became a vampire. He is sad and simple and holds a rose Anabella gave him the day she left. The rose is ageless, and a minor artifact from the goddess of love.

NPC Profile: A heartbroken maiden, who loves beautiful things and speaks in a sing-song voice. She misses her first love from sixty years prior.

Maurice: Init -2; Atk club -1 melee (1d4-1); AC 9; HD 1d4; MV 30'; Act 1d20; SV Fort -1, Ref -2, Will +2; AL L

6. The Cat Lord: A pounce of 1d100 normal cats comes to the tower and starts singing at midnight, serenading their imprisoned lord. It's possible some of these may wander to the tree and get into combat with the weskeebs. The cats will stay for 2d4 turns. If the PCs spend significant effort bonding with the cat they will earn 1d4 Luck points.

NPC Profile: The sleepy, mercurial cat lord never answers a question directly. He is attracted to shiny objects.

7. The Chaos Mage: A voice fills the air (coming from the image of the wizard on the tower) and commands, "Say, 'Helcore is the mightiest of all wizards', now you fools, or face my wrath!" PCs who do not comply will be targets from a burst of bone shards over 1d6 rounds. Each round, randomly pick who in the party gets attacked. A bone shard attack does 4d4+4 damage. PCs who make a successful DC 15 Reflex save will take half damage. Players who repeat the words "Helcore is the mightiest of all wizards" will not be attacked.

NPC Profile: Egotistical to the extreme, Helcore will steer every conversation about his exploits, which are many.

8. Ripears the Redcap: 8 redcaps appear pulling a cart with a catapult and several small barrels filled with blood. They demand the right to shoot the catapult at their brother, Ripears (all redcaps need blood to survive). If denied, they attack. If allowed, they will catapult five barrels into the tower. This will cause no damage to the building. After completing this task, they leave.

NPC Profile: A murderer who enjoys discussing his craft, and the virtues of blood.

Redcaps (8): Init +3; Atk wicked wounding knife +1 melee (1d4+wounding); AC 15; HD 2d8; hp 9 each; MV 40'; Act 3d20; SP Immune to charm, sleep, wounding knife (+1 additional damage per round, damage stacks), 50% magic resistance; SV Fort +2, Ref +4, Will +1; AL C.

A redcap is 2-foot-tall evil looking fae with pointed ears and a mouth filled with jagged teeth, which are too large for its face. Every Redcap wears a large red toboggan, colored by old blood.

9. Horned Skeleton with Gem Eyes: A horned skeleton warrior with gems for eyes bearing a flaming sword appears. It charges one of the warriors.

Horned Skeleton: Init +1; Atk longsword +7 melee (1d8+4); AC 15; HD 7d12; hp 43; MV 30'; Act 2d20; SP un-dead traits, half damage from piercing and slashing weapons; SV Fort +2, Ref +0, Will +0; AL C.

NPC Profile: An angry king, who killed his brothers to gain his crown. He's still furious he was tricked and trapped in the tower.

10. Witch with White Hair and Black Eyes: A large black crow flies around and lands near the PC who is the most Chaotic. The possessed crow introduces herself as Malpas via telepathy. Malpas promises she can bestow a wish if the PC helps the kobolds when they attack and try to break the binding magic of the tower. The crow is lying about the gift. (If this encounter is rolled, Random Die Drop Encounter no. 12 must occur later in the adventure.)

NPC Profile: A convincing liar that uses twisted logic to disparage the forces of Law.

Possessed Crow: Init +3; Atk beak +1 melee (1d3); SP telepathy; AC 13; HD 1d4; hp 2; MV fly 30'; Act 1d20; SV Fort +0, Ref +3, Will +1; AL C.

11. Efreet Female: The sky above the PCs opens and a female efreet cackles while shooting fiery rain down upon them. This attack causes 3d6 damage, (DC 14 Reflex save for half damage). The efreet departs after the first round she appears.

NPC Profile: This efreet hates men, due to being scorned by her former lover.

12. The Dragon Door: A group of 5d20 kobolds appear at the entrance to the property and are dazed for one round. On the next round they will charge the tower with ladders and grappling hooks (both used to help them cross the moat). These are the descendants of the tribe of kobolds that originally served the dragon that was bound to the tower to create the Dragon Door – Dreugzhoul the Dire Dragon. They have brought Foe Maegur- a hammer that can break the magic that holds their master in the tower. The hammer is a +1 warhammer, and strikes with a Dispel Magic as if cast by a 10th-level wizard every time it hits. Beyond this, the kobolds are normal.

If the kobolds are successful in their attack, the PCs will hear a dragon roar, and in the next round (and for 2d4 rounds) the dragon will emerge from the tower (removing the main entrance) and attack the PCs. If successful in destroying the PCs, the dragon will then attack the spot where it was bound – and strive to enter the tower.

Kobold (5d20): Init +1; Atk tiny sword -2 melee (1d4-1); AC 11; HD 1d2; hp 2; MV 20'; Act 1d20; SP infravision 100'; SV Fort -2, Ref +0, Will -2; AL N.

Dreugzhoul the Dire Dragon: Init +11; Atk claws +14 melee (1d8), bite +14 melee (1d12), tail slap +14 melee (1d20), wing buffet +14 melee (2d12); AC 29; HD 11d10; hp 99; MV 60'; Act 5d20 (melee)+1d20 (spells). SP dragon traits (see below), spells (check +3, comprehend languages); SV Fort +11, Ref +11, Will +11; AL C.

Special powers:

Dragon breath (3x day): Electricity based; damage equals dragon's hps, DC 21 Ref save for half; 1-4 line forks, width 5', total length 3d6 x 10'.

Dive bomb attack: When fighting from the air, the dragon's first round of claw and bite attacks receive an additional +4 attack bonus and +1d8 damage.

Hypnotic stare: The dragon can hypnotize targets with its gaze. The dragon can gaze into the eyes of one target per round by using one action die. A creature that meets the dragon's gaze must make a DC 20 Will save or stand stupefied as long as the dragon holds its gaze.

Clear passage (at will): The dragon can pass through vegetation without leaving any trace.

Earth to mud (1/hour): The dragon can transform an area of earth into sticky mud. The area transformed can be up to 50' x 50' in size. The mud, up to 3' deep, slows movement to half speed for all within.

Spider climb (at will): The dragon can climb any surface as if it were a spider.

NPC Profile: The dragon is sly, and desires to learn recent news and any information that will allow him to escape.

13. The Rat King: From the tower the sound of beautiful music starts playing. If anyone looks at the tower they see the Rat King playing six flutes. In 1d10 rounds, a group of 3d10 teenaged children walk up the tower path and jumps into the moat. The Rat King plays for 1d10+5 rounds. When the music ends the children run back to the streets, none wear ruby goggles.

NPC Profile: Exceptionally bored, the Rat King is hungry for conversation. He is also easily distracted, and argues with itself constantly.

14. Beautiful Woman: The ghost of a beautiful woman, Esselglam the Assassin, appears and with her gaze attempts to enslave the PC with the highest Personality in the party using a charm-like ability. If successful the ghost commands the PC to walk into the moat, if not the ghost attacks the PC.

Esselglam the Ghost: Init +2; Atk charm (single target within sight) or draining touch +6 melee (1d4 permanent physical ability score loss, PC choice); AC 10; HD 2d12; MV fly 40'; Act 1d20; SP un-dead traits, immune to non-magical weapons, charm (DC 15 Ref save to resist); SV Fort +2, Ref +4, Will +6; AL C.

NPC Profile: This former assassin misses killing, and will do her best to cause harm the PCs.

15. Halfling with No Eyes: A halfling named Bogo wearing goggles comes to the tower to sell candied eyeballs. He sells them for 4 gp. They look disgusting, but are delicious. If asked, he admits he collects eyeballs from dead beings, and uses a family recipe to make them into candy.

Bogo: Init -1; Atk dagger +1 melee (1d4); AC 12; HD 1d8; hp 4; MV 30'; SV Fort+1, Ref +2, Will +0; AL C.

NPC Profile: This halfling is obsessed with eyes, and will want to discuss the topic with any who will listen.

16. Female with Chaos Symbol Necklace: Aphelia, a young follower of Chaos arrives looking for converts. She has a high Intelligence and Personality, but no class abilities. For every member of the party she converts, she gains 1d4 cleric levels, instantly. New followers gain +1d6 on their next attack and damage roll. If she converts three PCs, a minion of Chaos will appear and offer each convert and Aphelia a boon. She will stay around for 3d4 rounds, and then disappear.

Aphelia: Init +0; Atk club +1 melee (1d4) AC 11; HD 1d8; hp 5; MV 30'; Act 1d20; SV Fort+1, Ref +0, Will +3; AL C.

NPC Profile: The being trapped in the tower is wise and a caustic critic of the force of Law. In truth this is Oya the Demigoddess of Change. She has forgotten her true nature when she was trapped in the tower. If she converts others to follow Chaos (through Aphelia) she has a chance of remembering her true nature (20% per being converted).

17. A Man with Glasses: A man named Olad visits the tower with a large barrel filled with water on wheels. He offers the PCs a chance to look into the barrel for 100 gp (per PC). Inside is a friendly Memory Turtle, when any being looks upon the turtle and fails a DC 13 Willpower save he becomes transfixed as the turtle's shell displays their fondest memories for 1d10 rounds. They also gain 3d4 temporary hit points and +1 to hit and damage for the next 24 hours. Those who make their saving throw briefly remember a fond memory and walks away melancholy for a round.

Olad: Init +0; Atk short sword +1 melee (1d6) AC 13; HD 1d8; hp 5; MV 30'; Act 1d20; SV Fort+1, Ref +1, Will +1; AL C.

NPC Profile: A sage and savvy merchant, he will offer advice on any topic related to business.

18. Man with a Dark Visage and Mysterious Symbol on his Head: Psychedelic colors fill the air with alien music. The PCs who fail a DC 13 Willpower save are filled with euphoria and get a hint on how to solve the next riddle. They also gain a +3 on any spell that attacks the mind for the next 24 hours. Those who make their saving throw are filled with sadness and crave the unearthly music for the rest of their days, but still gain a +1 on the next spell that attacks their mind within the next 24 hours.

NPC Profile: A friendly anarchist, who is often distracted because he is constantly day-dreaming.

19. Old Man with a Polyhedron: All PCs are filled with a vision of a great wizard god defeating hordes of un-dead. All PCs gain +3 on all rolls in their next 1d4 encounters.

NPC Profile: A master tactician, this old man will give excellent advice on any topic where such knowledge is useful.

20. Man with a Pipe: A bearded old man accompanied by a group of 12 dwarves and a halfling arrive seeking shelter. They look battered and will not disclose their names. No magic will compel them to share that information or the purpose of their travel. They pay for lodging in 100 ancient gold coins.

The next day after receiving shelter they leave. However, in the cottage they leave behind a magic acorn with a note that says, "All who wander are not lost! Thank you for the hospitality!" If the PCs are attacked while the dwarves and halfling are taking shelter in the cottage, they will not provide assistance. Nigella will likely be annoyed by the guests in the cottage.

The Magic Acorn: When thrown it explodes upon impact and does 6d6 fire damage in a 15' radius. Targets that make a DC 14 Reflex save take half damage.

NPC Profile: A humble genius, who has sage level knowledge of history, the old man is friendly although somewhat pedantic when giving advice.

Handout A

Dearest Yonaxis –
Next time I will be even nastier if you refuse my invitation...
(This poacher dared to try and steal one of my precious goats, so don't mourn his explosive passing!)

Shall we meet in a fortnight, at midnight, under the split willow? I will bring cheese – you bring the wine.
Infernally yours,
Horrible
Coven Mistress of the Blackest

Handout B

Lord of the Tower of Faces & Wizard Yonaxis:

In the name of the Regent, and The Invisible Council, you are hereby ordered to accept and imprison Xoxos the Malevolent, on the morrow, until which time The Regent or The Council needs the prisoner for questioning, or requires its execution.

Lord Alenkron,
Keeper of Harmony
& Sheriff of Naos

Handout C

Dearest Y.,

Thank you for giving me a personal tour of Naos. Here's something to brighten your life... just as you have my own.

Affectionately yours,
Lady Esmeralda

Handout D

LOG OF IDENTIFICATION & DIVINATION

REQUESTOR NAME | ITEM DESCRIPTION | FEE PAID

1.
2.
3.
4.
5.
6.
7.
8.
9.
20.
11.
12.
13.
14.
15.

Page 22

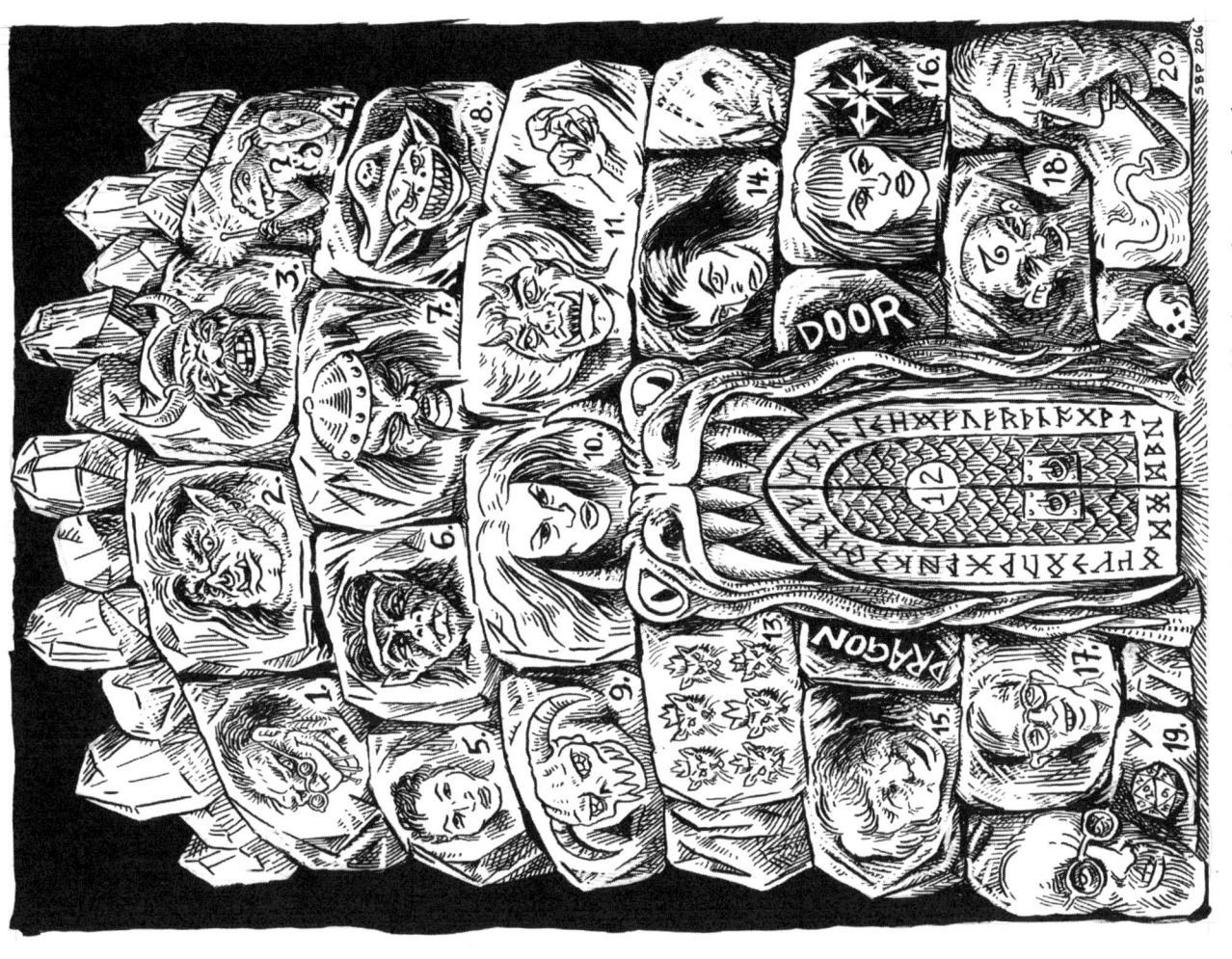

Download a larger version of the drop die table from this product's page at www.goodman-games.com

Handout E

ITEM	NOTES	PRICE
HONEYCAKES	(BAKERS DOZEN) CAKES MADE WITH HONEY EXTRACTED FROM THE WASPS OF ZANZIZAR	6,000 GP
BRONZE ANVIL	WEIGHT 167 STONE, LENGTH 25 KT, HEIGHT 11 KT, FACE WIDTH 4 KT, HARDY 1X1 KT, PRITCHEL 1X1 KT*	1,000 GP
MYRRH CANDLES	SEVEN CANDLES, 12 KT TAPERED HIGH, WHITE IN COLOR, WITH A BASE OF 5"	1,000 GP +1 PT. BLOOD

*Note in Naos, the unit of measurement for modest distances is King's Pinky Toe or KT for short.

(At the bottom of the satchel you will find 8,000 gold pieces to pay for the deliveries noted above)

Page 23

The Estate of Vonaxis the Magnificent

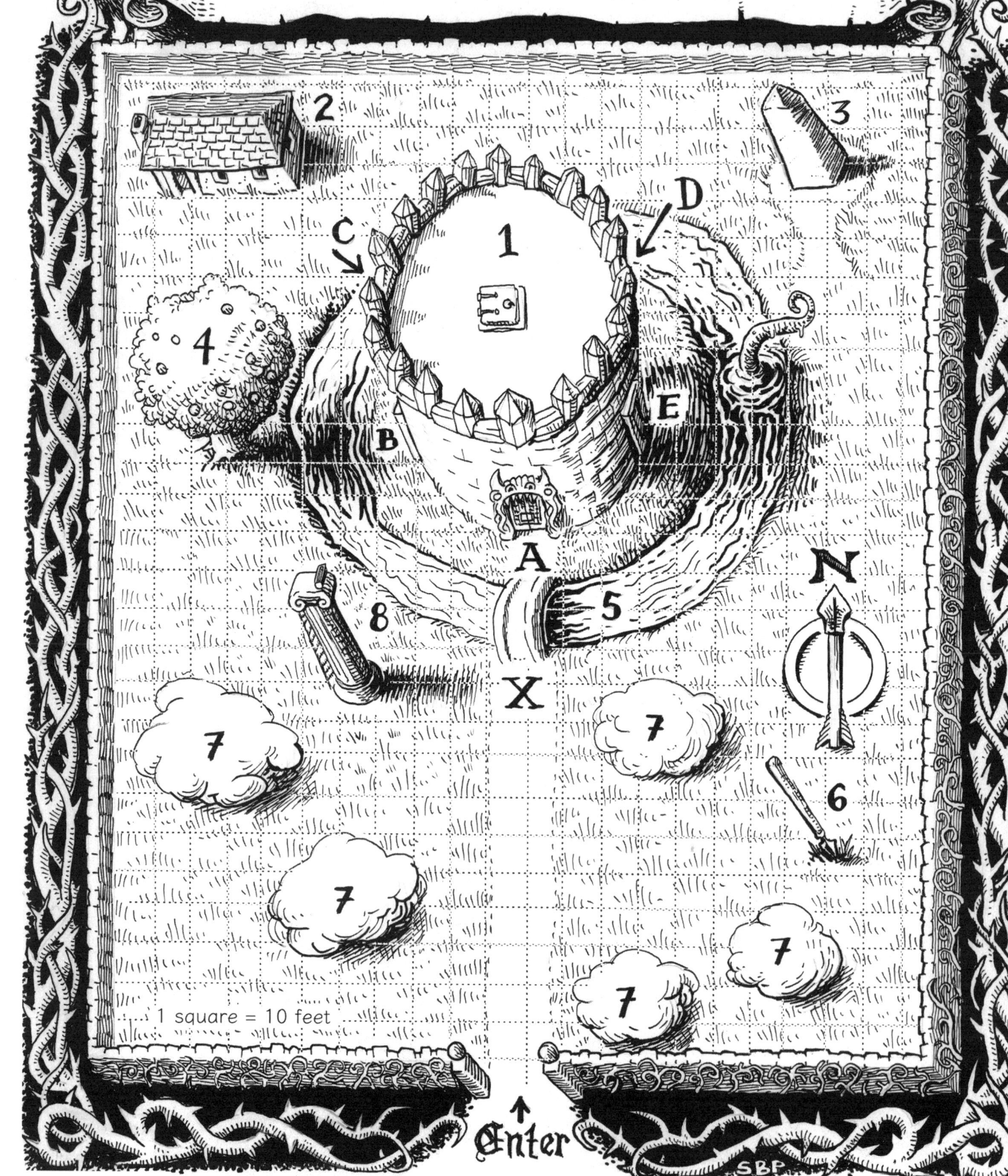

1 square = 10 feet

Enter